Adaline Hohf Beery

Poems of a Decade

Adaline Hohf Beery

Poems of a Decade

ISBN/EAN: 9783337408091

Printed in Europe, USA, Canada, Australia, Japan

Cover: Foto ©Andreas Hilbeck / pixelio.de

More available books at **www.hansebooks.com**

POEMS OF A DECADE

BY

ADALINE HOHF BEERY

HUNTINGDON PA
Published by the Author
1897

J. L. RUPERT, PRINTER
J. W. KING, BOOKBINDER

CONTENTS.

v

ix

I.

THROUGH THE YEAR.

SONG FOR THE NEW YEAR.

THE last low dirge o'er the buried year
   Floats off in the starless night;
   The cock-crow heralds the day-dawn keen,
  With gem-crusted hills of white;
The worn-out chorus the fresh air thrills,
  Forgot is their late lament;
A dash of life tints their melody,
  A rhythmic of glad hopes blent.

The windy moors, in a placid mood,
  Consent to the sun's caress;
The sheeted brook and the clear blue bay
  Are marked with the time's impress;
The new year's born! and along the scale
  Young hearts ring a jubilee
In tune with winds and their snow-freight pure,
  And kisses of cloud and sea.

Forget now troubles that had no name,
  And cease from your fret and haste;
The runes of nature have one refrain,—
  No hurry, no rest, no waste;
Strike chord with harps of sweet-tempered string
  That sound thro' the sky's blue wall;
Lay close your ear to the world's great heart,
  And sing as its needs may call.

NIGHT IN JANUARY.

SIFTING, sifting, 'gainst the panes,
Drifting, drifting, thro' the lanes,
Whitely falling thro' the darkness,
   Wilding flying down the air,
Gusts and caravans of snowflakes
   Sow a chillness everywhere.

Loudly, loudly, pipes the gale,
Proudly, proudly, leaves a trail
Paved with flags from crystal quarries,
   On the floors and window-sills;
Thrusts a blast thro' every crevice,—
   Biting breath of storm-swept hills.

Weary, weary, widows sigh,
Dreary, dreary, thoughts reply;
For the pillow's hard with sorrow,
   And the fire no longer glows;
Stray, perhaps, some breadless orphans
   Through the printless waste of snows.

Sweetly, sweetly, our loved rest;
Fleetly, fleetly, may our quest
Find a comfort for the wretched,
   Back to joy their faith recall;
We are each our brother's keeper,—
   God is Father of us all.

THE MARCH OF THE WHITE STORM.

WHEN the day woke up with leaden eyelids,
    Blinking with the sleep that pinned them fast,
    With surprise he found blithe winter fairies
Bringing ermine blankets on the blast.

Shrilly piped the gale around his pillow,
    Rudely shook a snow-shower on his cheek;
Rose he then, and looked across the landscape,
    Full of troops with hoofs and banners bleak.

Loudly rode the van into the morning,
    Praised with drums and trumpet-flourish keen;
Wildly shrieked the fifers up the valleys;
    Horse and foot impatient filled the scene.

Bravely streamed aloft the speckless ensigns,
    As the news of conquest sped to rear;
White-spurred cavalry and sheeted footmen
    Swept like outlaws by with long, mad cheer.

Blared anon the hoarse, twin-throated bugles,
    As the phantom army sacked the towns;
Brooks and lakelets masked their crystal faces,
    O'er which trailed its snow-embroidered gowns.

Leafless boughs set up their dreary dirges,
    Fireless chimneys wailed in weary rhyme,
Through the key-hole shot a mocking whisper,
    "Hark ye! this is winter's frolic time."

Endless marched the grim, white-lanced procession
    From the west, whose haunts storm-secrets keep;
Tired at last, the day let fall his curtains,
    Sighed "Good-night," and went again to sleep.

A MIDWINTER MORNING.

A STILL, white earth, with random foot-paths crossed,
  With drifted meadows brushed with soft gray mist,
    And trees which some night elfin must have kissed,
Whose breath congealed to bristling pikes of frost;
A touch, and hair and robe and feet are mossed
  Like some pale miller powdered with his grist;
    This keen white bower is sure a lovers' tryst,
Whose thoughts the scene with purity embossed.
The storm's forgotten in this quiet walk,
  The gale is dead, the sun but "bides a wee";
All flakes on bough and bramble sweetly talk
  Of white-souled truth, the heart of God's decree;
So should our lives be garmented and grand,
The crowning work of his perfecting hand.

A MARCH CARNIVAL.

A ROSELIT smile had blushed o'er wood and hill,
  When, loth to leave, the sun had said "good-
    night";
Round Luna promised guard, but dim her light.
Earth sighed, and slept. But ere the dawn a thrill
Uneasy woke her. Then a deepening chill
  Wreaked moans from out the forest; the moon's flight
  Was hid by sullen, steely clouds; a blight
Of blinding snow and cutting sleet the still
Of morning struck; a piping gale flung scoff
  Broadcast, and with harsh dalliance pressed in haste
A crystal chaplet on the oak's bare brow.
Adown the glen it chased the songbirds off
  And nipped the crocus buds; a jeweled waste
The frolic left: O March, a despot thou!

6

GALES.

WITH Southern pride and bluster
　　The sudden breezes bring
The passing bell of winter,
　　The birth-night of the spring.
The air is hoarse with bugles,
　　With fifes and kettle-drums;
With all this tragic prelude
　　The ballad singer comes.

The play of March commences;
　　The stage is wildly dressed
With smoke and hail of battle,
　　And gleam of sun-tipped crest;
The rush of stalwart victors
　　The trumpets' clangor swells,
And no one hears the vespers
　　Of distant village bells.

But soon the din is silent;
　　The drum has ceased to beat,
The broken ranks, in panic,
　　Before a queen retreat;
Her breath dispels the tumult,
　　Her eye reflects blue sky,
Her hand the war-marks covers,
　　Her foot trips softly by.

But chief her voice hath magic
　　The spirit to enthrall;
She sings an old, old ditty
　　But sweeter yet than all;
The world grows rapt and dreamy
　　Beneath her siren strain;
Her bonny face is welcome,—
　　All joys are in her train.

7

THE TURN-COAT.

YOU naughty March! how could you cheat me so?
    But yesterday you took me in your lap,
    And kissed me on both cheeks; but in the night
Some bad dream must have stirred your passion up,
For now you're cold and furious toward me.
What have I done? Come, sit here in the sun,
And lookly me kindly in the eyes again,
And tell me why you scowl and bluster so?
And do you strike me with an icicle?
For shame!   I'll go indoors and wipe my tears.

THE AWAKENING.

O SAD-EYED April,
      In womanish tears,
    What sorrow burdens
      Thy youthful years?
Or is't but joy?   I half believe that smile
Was born of gladness, tho' of briefest while.

    Thy feathered heralds
        At peep of day
    Shake off the rain-drops
        With matins gay;
The choral throng possess the budding woods,
And make thee laugh, to spite thy somber moods.

    Thy showers impulsive
        Were not amiss;
    Ne'er emerald carpet
        Was soft as this;
The fresh young johnny-jump-ups fragrance fling,
And brooks and falls a royal lyric sing.

8

O, joyous April,
　　I hail thy birth!
Thy benediction
　　Renews the earth.
If, thro' with death and winter, in the sky
My soul shall bloom, I do not fear to die.

AN APRIL PROSPECT.

YE solemn, silent hills! out of your sleep
　　I see ye've quivered, and a blush of green
　　Tints your brown bosom, and your tangled locks
Bristle with expectation of new sheen.
Your mother wept because ye looked so dead,
And to the river ye have cradled long
Her swift tears ran, and angered the fair stream.
And then she answered rough, and frightened you
With lash and glare; but with true mother-heart
Her rage soon blew away, and then she smiled
On you, dear hills, and ye laughed back again.
E'en now ye're throwing kisses to the sun,
Who loves you too, great sweetheart of the world.
I count your coronets from this airy view,
And claim you kin, for ye have never changed
Since I was born, but yearly wrap your cloak
Around your bonny shoulders with the same
Blithe grace, inviting me to old-time chat.
Stanch have ye stood, and ye shall stand for aye,
Emblem of truth that dureth thro' all wrecks.

9

UNFETTERED.

LOOK at you yellow, laughing sun! How soft
And exquisite the first deep breath of spring!
It rained a little in the night; and now
The steaming roofs and cackling barn-yards tell
Of things unloosed from Winter's icy locks.

How huddled up in snowy gloom we were!
Old Boreas with monotonous vigor piped
Thro' tiniest crevice, whom the hungry fire
Half vainly fought, and we by turns reproached.
The garden slept 'neath flaky feather-beds;
The brown boughs sheltered not a single bird;
The streets rang dull against their leaden roof;
The soul of all out-doors seemed stark and dead.

But now! do look how shines the very air;
And in the small black pools beside the road
The glorious sun his faithful likeness pours.
The cold banks in the hollows of the hills
Are trickling thro' the glens where daffodils
Are pulling off their winter hoods to catch
The robin's first sweet note of wild delight.

O, Spring! I feel like skipping down the walk,
So free and fresh my spirit leaps to-day.
Now I begin to think of sprouting seeds,
And knobby trees, and grass-blades swift unsheathed,
And pink sunrises, golden noons, and eves
With purple habit thick with stars besprent.

And yet, these are not thee, my subtle spring;
They of thy presence are but cheerful signs;
Invisible and indescribable,
Thy spirit scatters its compelling charm,
And unto yearly resurrection brings
Grass, flower, and tree, praise, love, content, and hope,
Out of the bleakness of a frost-bound world.

SPRING NIGHT.

THE house is dull and close,
  Tiresome the lamp's warm glare;
Come forth into the night,
  Into this sweet, wide air.

The sounds of day are dead,
  Save as the passing scream
Of mettled iron steed
  Breaks on the starlit dream.

From marsh and brook and pond
  Wells up a steady drone
From glad bass throats, to join
  The river's monotone.

The moon is late tonight,
  And Venus wears a veil;
Stray vapors sweep the sky
  With long and stately trail.

The atmosphere's divine;
  All sense drinks in the charm;
The soul throbs in its cage,
  Moved by an unseen arm.

The tides of various moods
  Blend in one surge of love;
Our thoughts unconscious drift
  Toward the deep above.

O, witchery of Spring!
  We quaff thy nectared bowl;
We clasp this night to heart,
  And wrap it in our soul.

11

THE DOMINANT.

I WAKE one yellow daybreak
  With a sun-spot on my cheek;
Methinks I hear some fairy
  With soft persuasion speak;
I peep between the curtains;—
  Out in the fresh, young glow
A robin's rich soprano
  Rings in to me, "Hello!"

Hard by the back veranda
  The bare, black cherry trees,
With straight, long-fingered shadows,
  The morning's spirit seize;
Among their long-stiff branches
  Swings Æolus to and fro,
And with his kiss imprinted
  The gauntlet flings, "Hello!"

I walk out in the garden
  Where black clods sweating lie;
A dainty breakfast spying,
  Old chanticleer struts by;
His family around him,
  Each with a worm in tow,
He nods his satisfaction,
  And stammers, "Ho-o-hello!"

Down to the sheeny mill-pond,
  Close to its reedy rim,
I stroll with airy footstep,
  Framing a springtide hymn;
From fifty throats in discord,
  Hid in the water low,
There comes, in cheerful gurgle,
  The selfsame note, "Hello!"

And so the spell is on me;
  Which way I step or look
Some sprite persists in filling
  With music every nook;
I know her! let my gladness
  In foolish riot go;
I'll throw my arms around her,
  And cry, "Dear Spring, hello!"

AN OUT-DOOR SYMPHONY.

SOFT-SANDALED thro' the woodland aisles I pass,
    Marking the bough-laced roof, and vistas dim
    And fretted lights, and oaken pillars grim
Leaf-draped, with floor of smooth and fragrant grass.
Bursts in a silvery tide a thrilling mass
  From the high galleries; the happy brim
  Of song o'ertilts in loyal birdhood's hymn,`
Spilling their notes like beads of sparkling glass.
A solemn choral echoes thro' the dell
  As thro' Pan's pipes the rising storm-wind plays,—
A minor prelude to quick notes that swell
  Into a dirge of sobbing rain;—a blaze
Of sunshine quickly hints a change of key,
And skylark's joy drops down the airy sea.

13

THE VANGUARD.

"APRIL showers bring May flowers,"
So the rhythmic adage goes;
Rain and sunshine deftly mingled
Woo the shyest bud that blows.

Now at last we've counted over
All the days of fitful skies;
Mayday dawns in perfect glory,
Laughing from a hundred eyes.

Buttercups and dandelions,
Jaunty in their yellow coats,
Meadows waving o'er with cowslips
Like a fleet of fairy boats;

Violets in bunches growing,
Twisting necks in playful strife;
Mountains pink with sheeted laurel,
All the world with beauty rife.

Birds atilt in highest tree-tops
Pouring from their songful throats
Matins, madrigals and vespers,
Medley of divinest notes.

Every song has spring-time flavor;
And the serried bloom of May
Bristling with its points of color
Tells us summer's on the way!

WILL IT LAST?

'TIS morning in a summer world;
   Young Phoebus' wain spurs thro' the gate
With crimson banners far unfurled,
   Tracking with gifts his march of state;
The dew-hung leaves stir with delight;
   The birds, night-bosomed in the oak,
Storm thro' the grove in wild song-flight,
   Rethreading trills the darkness broke.

The air—O, inexpressible!
   So soft, and sweet, and daintily blue,
   So washed with perfume and with dew,
Rising from every flower-bell;
'Tis ecstasy! we almost float,
   All senses bound by beauty's sway;
   Could it but stay one whole round day,
Unbroke by one discordant note! .

They say that heaven is such a place,
   Perfect in grace of fountains, flowers,
Rivers, which stately trees embrace,
   Music, pervading fruit-hung bowers;
But O, the thought is most too much:
   Can these things be forever so?
Let me the rim of heaven but touch,
   And I shall prove that faith doth know.

AFTER THE SHOWER.

THE night has fallen upon the hills;
   The light breeze kisses the tear-wet leaves;
A drift of perfume the fresh air fills,
   And birds are crooning beneath the eaves.

The cool town nestles in peace below;
   The buzz of business no more is seen;
The frogs are having a merry go
   Down by the shallows, embanked with green.

The moon's coquetting with drifting clouds;
   Thro' my open casement she sometimes peeps;
A tide of pleasure my being crowds,
   My unlit chamber the night balm sweeps.

Hard by in a chapel a hymn I hear;
   With nature mingles its harmony;
From a neighboring doorstep, resounding clear,
   A boy's young treble floats out to me.

The flashing street lights illume the lawn;
   I turn, and kindle my yellow flame;
The spell is broken, the rare gloom gone;
   My books and pictures are idly tame.

The light has gathered a choir indoors
   Of June bugs bumping along the wall;
Their awkward drone in my tired ear pours,
   And witched with slumber my eyelids fall.

CLOUD FANTASIES.

UP from the west stream rays of billowed whiteness
    On sapphire ocean edged with paler blue;
  But momently the vapors grow in brightness,
    Touched with a brush of glad and changeful hue;
The great gold orb upon his rim reposing
  With amber sheen the purple overlays;
Far Orient phantoms, dimpled arms disclosing,
  Blush into rose at the old lover's praise.

Dark, tattered shapes proclaim the night advancing,
  And dim and mellow grows the afterlight;
Upon the scene the half-grown moon comes dancing,
  With coronet of silvery stars bedight.
The graceful fleeces east-bound now are speeding,
  At morning tryst to meet the freshened sun;
In soft confusion from the sky receding,
  They leave clear silence, and the play is done.

SEPTEMBER.

IN Quaker livery the mists enfold
  The river's bosom and the mountain's head,
  And turn young Phœbus' cheek from dashing red
To hazy white; but soon a flood of gold
Dries up the fog, and every prospect bold
  Stands out in balmy glory; like the tread
  Of angels clouded fantasies o'erspread
The azure plain, in phantom files enrolled.
After a sunset miracle, and thrush
  And lark with autumn vespers fill the trees,
Night's stately queen deepens the twilit hush,
  While fairy whispers grow from dying breeze:
"Come, sprites, scatter the star-dust o'er the sky;
Live while you live; September soon will die."

SEPTEMBER VOICES.

BENEATH September's blue and amber flush
  The full-fed river, by the sun caressed,
Blends like an anthem with the noontide hush,—
  A hint of song and source alike unguessed.

    A troop of gay maidens
      Eyes gray, black, and blue,
    With hair many-colored,
      Comes flocking in view;
    "In praise of September,
      The golden," they sing;
    And into the forest
      Their music they bring.

The south wind rocks the dawn-kissed leaves
  That droop, in tender shade,
Above a pair of cradled birds,
  With pillows moss inlaid;
It croons a charmful lullaby
  Out of the starlit night,
Or whispers in their waking ears,
  "Up, for a sun-bath bright!"

Dews are falling on the clover
    Meadows low;
Milkmaids calling old rhymes over
    Sing them so:
"Come, my beauties, turn your feet;
Though I know the clover's sweet,
Haste your mistress dear to meet;
    Co,' boss, co'!"

What wild confusion's this
  That racks the dusky air?
The strident chorus wakes
  The thickets everywhere;

Some Pandora's
    Sprung the lid:
"Katy didn't!
    Katy did!"

A hint of the summer departing
  Grows clearer with every new dawn;
And faintly the autumn's suggestion
  Creeps on after sunset is gone;
O, joyous, bewitching September,
  May memory be faithful to keep
Thy pure, perfect days thro' the bleakness
  When nature has gone to her sleep.

IN THE DUSK.

THERE is no moon; the scattered stars are dim,
  But thro' the broken banks of cloud uprolls
In various harmony a vesper hymn.
  Its soft, full notes, like breath of fervent souls
Free passage finds 'mid seas of blazing balls
  To heaven's own heart, where Light and Power sit,
And harpers throng the royal music halls.
  Now from a row of windows gaily lit
A swell of instruments delights the air;
  With steady beat the band discourses loud,
With cornet's playful tune, and martial blare
  Of bugles, and of drums a sturdy crowd.
Across the lawn a mellow organ strain
  Pours lightly, soothingly; a girlish voice
Floats on the waves of rhythm in low refrain,
  And in the gloom our listening hearts rejoice.
Close by breaks forth a witching violin
  In graceful fantasy; but every sound
Dies presently, except the cricket's din
  That rends the ear of darkness all around.

19

OCTOBER FIRST.

THE month came in with visage half a-cloud,
  As if to doubt what welcome were in store,
  But cleared her face to greet the sun betimes
And fanned us with her pure autumnal breath.
We praised her, and for tokens of her reign
Scanned the green woods; some scattering yellow tops
Told the sure sign that summertide was gone.
She looked abroad herself, and as in grief
At her own triumph, dropped a gentle tear;
Like as a child, with eyes o'erfull of tears
And one drops down in sight, bursts into sobs,
She fell to fitful weeping; with a moan
Caught by the western wind, she called across
The summer to her sister April, born
Of clouds, and kissed her sympathetic cheek.
Some comfort must have filled her from that touch,
For smiles broke through and we rejoiced again.
We studied trees to deck our canvas with;
A dash of red upon a shower of gold,
With sunglints on their diamonded leaves.
A roll of mist soon dulled the living tints,
But amber sky peeped through horizon rifts,
And bade us wait the sunset after rain.
Lo! ere the dark another fretful burst
Wrung all the trees and bushes, and they wept
And sighed together, making common grief.
October! lift thy head upon the hills;
Thy beauty is the triumph of the year;
Mourn not that robe so rich shall fade and fall,
For out of it shall spring the happy green
That crowns next May-day with its keen delights.

ON THE BEACH.

A SOFT September twilight draped the sea;
   In pensive monotone, among the piers
   The breakers roared, and dashed their briny tears
Back on its bosom; silence fell on me,
Standing alone upon the sands; the free,
   Wide water with an anthem filled my ears,
   Ringing a prelude to th' eternal years
That, boundless, deep, and grand, in heaven shall be.
Along the dim horizon swept a sail
   That vanished soon; a flock of gulls flew by,
      Catching my transient notice; ceased the moan
Of rushing wave one instant, while a trail
   Of moonlight quivered o'er it; then the sky
      Was blank: the sea and I held tryst alone.

DAYBREAK.

A MIST hangs over the meadow,
   A hoarfrost sharpens the air;
The tops of the village steeples
   Disrobe for a mantle more fair.

The Orient flings up a glory—
   A rose-cloud embroidered with gold;
It shines on the upper heaven,
   Which star-spangled draperies fold.

The motionless maples and poplars
   Their turn for the warm light await,
And lastly, late daisies and grasses
   Wake up to their gem-stiffened state.

Hail, miracle-worker, day-god!
   Who breaks the broad bars of the night,
Thy empire is dearer than Luna's,
   Tho' dotted with blossoms of light.

A PERFECT DAY.

OUT of the South, where puffs of sun-white cloud
   The pale blue hangings of the heaven emboss,
   The warm wind blows the crimson woods across,
And half-forgotton ripples tell aloud
The gladness of the brooks, which float a crowd
   Of leaves, like autumn navies; on the moss,
   Fit couch for dreaming ease, the grave oaks toss
Their acorns, and the banks in shadow shroud.
The half-blown moon is limned against the west,
   A lingerer to witness this pure day;
Who knows, when she pursues the stars to rest,
   What sweeter smiles may charm her night away?
This is a day when joy flows to the brim,—
The stately echo of a summer hymn.

OCTOBER SNOW.

THE east glowed like a blush-rose fair,
   As Phœbus' wheels drove up the air;
   But murky banners trailed behind,
   Blown like a full sail by the wind.

At noon a gust of feathered rain
   A hornpipe danced without the pane,
   Then nestled blithely 'mid the leaves
   Whose gold and garnet brushed the eaves.

The green grass took a daintier shade,
   As the gay phantoms on it played;
   Gray vistas with their mirth grew dim
   And earth and sky blent at their rim.

As day declined the storm waxed brave;
   The blast a wintry warning gave;
   A thickening sheet earth's bosom spanned,
   And moonless night crept o'er the land.

NOVEMBER.

A T the altars in the groves
  Nature's priests do minister;
Up and down the transept throng
 Devotees who worship her;
She's in somber mood to-day,
For the madcap winds, in play,
  Rent her autumn robe in shreds,
  Strewed them o'er the fall-rose beds,
Left her gowned in simple gray,
Robbed her splendid jewel-tray,—
  Thoughtless urchins they!

Leafy brooks in ferny dell,
 Kissing pebbles as they purl,
Move in measure low and slow,
 Round in pensive eddies whirl;
Everywhere the tale's rehearsed:
How Queen Nature's court-elves durst
  In such topsy-turvy glee
  Snatch the crown from every tree,
Float them at the river's brink—
What could loyal subjects think?

Now she's weeping; and her tears
 Down the river's bosom run;
And the pulsing river's heart
 Swells in deep-toned unison;
All the air is full of sighs;
Quavering vespers wake replies
In the rafters of the skies;
  South-bound swallows, in gay rout,
  Turn their spring home inside out,
Thread with song their viewless track,
Vanish with their song, alack!
Till some green day brings them back.

At the altars in the groves,
    At the shrines amid the vales,
Still we kiss Queen Nature's robe,
    Though o'er rifled fields it trails.
'Tis a choir of sturdy throats
Flinging now their storm-wild notes
    Through the galleries of the year,—
    Hill, and wood, and summer mere.
'Tis the prelude, shrill and bold,
To the stately winter old,
        Stark, and stern, and cold.

A WALK IN INDIAN SUMMER.

THE country road, with fringing weeds and sod,
    Leads idly in the mellow morning sun
    Through yellow fields whose empty husks are spun
With fairy gossamer; nipped daisies nod
Ungraceful to the faded golden-rod,
    And trees, in somber habit like a nun,
    Sigh that their reign of bloom so soon is done,
And furrows mark where late the plowman trod.
The distant spires are thinly veiled in haze
    That hangs its purple folds upon the air;
The far-off pines the winds forever praise
    For strength and greenness which the year outwear;
The day lies like a message on the heart—
"Take joy; this peace is but of heaven a part."

A CHRISTMAS ORATORIO.

DINGLE, dingle,
　　Sleigh-bells chime,—
　Concious jingle
　Of a time
When an infant
　Pure as God
Found a cradle
　Ou the sod.

Blithe the wind of morn
　Tidings from the sky,—
"A Redeemer born!"—
　Brings, and frolics by.
Snowflakes kiss each other
　Dancing down the air,
Fall and melt to dewdrops
　On that pillow rare.

Now the frosty church bells wake!
　And so mighty is the tale
Which they tell, the echoes break
　Scarcely in the clouds:—"All hail!"
Bell to bell repeats the greeting,
　Emulous to ring it best;
Dome and steeple make obeisance
　To the royal baby Guest.

Long to common praise accustomed, now
　Breath the thousand pipes with wilder glee,
Weaving song-wreaths for that hallowed brow,
　Twining with the choir's full jubilee.
Harp and organ, lute and cornet blending,
　Stir to homage proudest hearts of earth;
Human-voiced, the choral of the ages
　Celebrates the wondrous Christ-child's birth.

On Judea's dusky plain
  Careful shepherds vigil keep;—
Suddenly a marvelous strain
  Bursts from out the starry deep:
With the Lord's descending angel
  Sweeps a rush of winged song
From the shining bards above him,
  Praising God,—a loyal throng.

    Sing the morning stars
      In a cosmic rhyme,
    Ringing in the bars
      Of the chant sublime;
  "Glory in the highest,"
      Swells and swells again,
  "Peace to all the nations,
      And good-will to men!"

      "Jubilate,"
        Every land!
      "Jubilate,"
        Chorus grand!
      "In excelsis
        Deo laus;"
      Speed the message
        Zones across!

BIRDS IN THE SNOW.

WHERE do you come from, brown little coats?
Where did you learn your quick, cheery notes?
Though flies the snow on midwinter wind,
Out in your bare feet you never mind.

Chirp, chirp away, dear birds in the snow!
Sing us a lesson out of the snow;
Happy, no matter what weathers come,
Trusting our Lord for each daily crumb.

We have our fireside, safe from the storm;
Wrapped in our furs, we're cosy and warm;
Hopping about on tree-branches bare,
You sing away with never a care.

We fret and grumble, tho' days are fine,
Tho' every day with plenty we dine;
Brown little birds, teach us your content.
That we may live as our Father meant.

27

II.

BECAUSE OF LOVE.

A VALENTINE.

TAKE, sweetheart,
This faint whisper of my yearning;
    All the verse of vulgar art
    Illy paints the love me burning;
        Turn thy dewy-lidded eyes
        On my homage, nor disguise
            Thy true soul;
            If thy dole
Sprinkle with affection meager,
    Yet I beg the morsel rare;
Never grew a plant more eager
    For a breath of sunlit air;
Like a church with ivies twined
            Thou art shrined
By my soul's caressing fingers;
    Not content to dwell afar,
Round thy radiant presence lingers
    My desire; I pray thee, bar
    Eyes that speak so tenderly
            Not from me!

31

ETUDE.

MY love sings like the mavis
    All in tune;
Her voice trills through the gamut
    Of all June.

Her eyes are star-time sapphires
    Set in dew;
I think the brook's low laughter
    Brims them too.

Her ears like ocean-shell pinks
    Brightly blush;
She hears the choirs of cloudland
    At eve's hush.

Her tresses fling defiance
    To the sun;
She's blossom, bird, and fairy
    Blent in one.

Her lips, like twin carnations
    But half-blown,
I've pressed, in love's emotion,
    To my own.

Her hand is like a leaf-touch,
    But a thrill
Enchains me when I feel it
    Speak her will.

Her soul is like the Alpine
    Edelweiss;
Her steel-true heart is to me
    Shield from vice.

My love's the contemplation
    Of my life;
I lay all gifts before her,—
    She's my wife!

A MAY MADRIGAL.

HITHER, thither,
  Floats the breeze;
Everywhither
  Drone the bees;
Like a witching maiden,
  Garlanded and shy,
May, with sweet airs laden,
  Makes her lovers sigh.

Birds are mating,
  Wed with song;—
No sad waiting
  In that throng;
Trees in full leaf-draping
  Whisper bough to bough;
Some stray tones escaping
  Tell me, "Woo her now!"

Come, love, wander
  Thro' the glen,
The spring yonder
  Drink again;
When we walked together
  Here so long ago,
'Twas in golden weather
  'Mid the autumn's glow.

In thy beaming
  Glances, sweet,
I sit dreaming
  At thy feet;
Waits for thee a castle
  In my heart unseen;
Let me by thy vassal,
  Thou my regnant queen!

SUNRISE ON THE HILLS.

THE stars are set; and from the sky
   A-shimmer with a golden dawn
Pale rose-tints top the hills which lie
   Far on the western landscape drawn;
The vale still sleeps; but on yon height
   The woodland choir the air awakes;
The echoes chase the drowsy night,—
   The sun upon earth's bosom breaks!

Hail thee, sweet sun! whose message glad
   My heart with love and rapture thrills;
Wake, soul! with doubt and discord sad,
   And greet the sunrise on the hills!

Thy path is swift, O god of day!
   To other eyes thou art but set;
Tell me of her, my love, I pray,
   Who in the twilight muses yet;—
What said she when the purple hills
   Caught the star-twinkling robe of night?
My heart with restless ardor fills;—
   Sent she no word, O courier bright?

O, merry sun, thy face is true,
   Thy hopeful light my being thrills;
Fail not thy trust; nor change the hue
   Of love which lies beyond thy hills!

I would not grieve thee, lover brave;
   A loyal swain deserves good news;
This wish to me thy lady gave:—
   "O, sun, thy service I would choose;
When thou hast crossed yon mountain high,
   Carry to him who owns my heart
This word: ' 'Twould be a softer sky
   Were thou and I no more apart!' "

O, gracious sun! my true love waits,
   Her heart for me with longing thrills;
Open the rosy morning gates
   And let me pass beyond the hills!

ANTICIPATION.

THE gold sun droops; the weary tale
   Of long, like days is almost summed;
The feathered peoples of the air
   Their song in my dull ears have drummed;
The shrouded skies trailed heavily
   Across the restless, hill-girt town;
And on my solitude the wings
   Of sweet, late memories settled down.

But now the sun but threads the gate
   To light its eastern side full soon,—
The side where swift my lover comes
   To greet me at the royal noon!
Ah, quicker throb the chords of love
   Upon the strings within my heart;
Two tides of joy will be, I know,
   More full for having been apart.

35

SING ME SOME TENDER STRAIN.

SING me some tender strain
   Whispering of love,
Love true as yonder stars
   Shining above;
Tell me you cherish me
   Deep in your heart,
That you will care for me
   Till death us part.

Sing low and gently, dear,
   While the day falls;
Song floats so sacredly
   Thro' night's dim halls;
Let notes of nesting birds
   On zephyr's wing,
With drowsy brooklet's purl,
   Join while you sing.

Love like a river wild,
   Noble and free,
Heeding no bank or fret
   Bounds to the sea;
So let your passion, dear,
   Come to my heart,
Blend with its restless depths
   With true love's art.

Teach me the lesson sweet
   Love only knows,—
Dearer is others' weal,
   Soothed my own woes;
Lighter the trouble is,
   Shorter the grief;
Sweet balm of Gilead—
   Love's own relief!

So let our wedded souls
    Live each for each,
Leave but earth's paradise
    Heaven's to reach !
There may our spirits sing
    Where God doth shine;
His love will perfect us,—
    Make ours divine.

CUPID AMONG THE BLOSSOMS.

O'ER the velvet-tufted carpet
In the still and happy orchard
Decked for nature's spring-time nuptials,
Four light feet went softly straying.
Two fair forms cast scarce two shadows
As the soft sun smiled upon them,
Peeping thro' the sprays of blossoms.

O, the air with perfume breathing!
O, the trees in wedding garments!
Overhead, the apple branches,
Thick with blooms of blushing petals,
Arched, and met with dainty rustle,
Laughed, and shook a fragrant shower
On the heads of youth and maiden
Dreaming, thinking naught of danger.

Temptingly, a spray of peach pink
Drooped and brushed the maiden's tresses;
Quickly he, with blue eyes tender,
Plucked the branch and wove it deftly
In her hair of wavy auburn;
Looked, and caught her eyes of hazel.

Ah, the sprite hid in those blossoms!
Never laid he plot more cunning!
Now the maiden's heart a-quiver
With the shaft the fearless archer
Aimed and shot, with stronger beatings
Filled her face with bright carnations;
Drooped her eyes, with shy protesting;
But the arrow wound was fatal.

Never looked the sky so sunny;
Never seemed the air so balmy;
Never knew she such a hero
As this one, so true and blue-eyed.
And the blossoms saw and listened,
Crowned the heads of youth and maiden,
Sealed their love with God's own signet.

TO-MORROW.

WAIT yet, O patient heart,
Till one more sun shall bloom upon the hills;
Smother the throb, whose depths, with mystic art,
Love fills!

The days are long and trite
While he is absent, and no voice can rouse
My soul like memoried whispers breathed one night—
His vows!

I shall be folded soon
In arms that pledged their shelter round my life,
Whose hands would lead me into shine of noon—
His wife!

O, if my love should die,
Or could no more return, then, Father, just
But kind, my bosom's broken tendrils tie
With trust.

DAY-DREAMING.

INTO the gray dawn, sown with pale stars,
Looks forth a maiden through window bars;
Naught in the landscape fixes her eye;
Off to the daybreak her fancies fly.

The day's dull duties her hands employ,
But 'neath her lashes shines out a joy;
She heeds not chatter of busy birds,
Nor finds her gladness in idle words.

Her heart is absent on some love quest,
Only in *his* eyes to find its rest.
If her skilled fingers to music turn,
She finds no lesson but love's to learn.

In long-drawn sweetness the trembling tones
Weave a soft heart-song that binds the zones;
If sunlight kisses her thoughtful brow,
His memoried glances caress her now,

The breeze is vocal with tender airs,
And white clouds sailing picture her prayers;
When sunset banners trail o'er the sea,
The low waves murmur, "He comes to thee!"

Ah, yes! to-morrow, perhaps, her dream
Will find full waking in love's full gleam;
So in the starlight, 'neath solemn oaks,
A benediction her heart invokes:

"O, faithful heavens, let your pure light,
In angel garments, guard him to-night!
With virtue's lilies bestrew his way,
And bring him to me when glows the day!"

CARMEN.

SAY, little robin red,
  Why dost thou sing
Matins so tenderly
  When dawns the spring?
Vespers scarce quiet thee,
  So glad thy breast,
Building the livelong day
  For two, thy nest.

Wind of the southern land,
  What sweet strains float,
Borne on thy dew-kissed wings,
  Tuned to bird's note?
Swinging on leafy boughs,
  With shy, quick grace,
Two little robins red
  Laugh in thy face.

"Mystery wonderful!"
  Whispers the bird;
"Learned, tho' by masters taught
  Never a word;
Love no reminder needs
  What time to glow,
Save our own hearts; my mate,
  Is it not so?"

"Spring is Love's wedding time,"
  Echoes the wind;
"This is my wedding march,
  Love's home to find;
Yon vocal forest aisles,
  Whither I go,
Hold fast the mystery;
  Come, and thou'lt know!"

40

Voices of wind and bird
   Into the wood
Drew me to fathom it.
   Lo! as I stood
Waiting, with dreamy eyes,
   A maid—a queen—
Captured my heart and said,
   "Love it must mean!"

TO-MORROW—SIX YEARS AFTER.

BE still, lone heart of mine,
  Till yonder day-star burnish one more noon;
  Into thy depths the smile of love shall shine
    So soon!

   All thro' the chilly spring
I've watched for daffodils, then blossom-drift,
Then *roses:*—to what fluttering soul they bring
    Their gift!

   Back in one other June
I took with him the wedding sacrament;
To-night I'll see him by a spirit-moon
    Dream-sent.

   For he is on the way
To me! Let not an anxious shadow dim
My precious prospect of a perfect day
    With him!

III.

INTROSPECTION.

MY TABERNACLE.

LOOPINGS of blue tether the ample sweep
  Of purple curtains, that shut in my soul
  To priestly service; with a golden bowl
Brimming with odorous prayer, in reverence deep
I part the trembling veil, whose shadows keep
  Hid from gross gaze the place where I am sole
  And mitered minister, with broidered stole,
And all my being in God's presence steep.

The outspread wings of cherubim o'ershade
  My heart; the voice of the Adored is heard
Blessing my gift of broken deeds; I'm paid
  For costliest offering with His simple word.
So shall this booth my sweetest refuge be,
Till one of "many mansions" opes for me.

UNUSED.

THE sun has risen and set another day;
  All day it strode, with summer strength, along
  Its shining race-course, and fulfilled its task.
The wild birds sang their song, and clove the sky
Upward, to catch approval from their God.
The river, sent on errand fruitful, flowed
Serenely faithful thro' the woods and meads.
The bees, whose instinct scoured the clover-fields,
Bro't with the eve their recompense of toil.
The flowers, with sweet, bright eyes, looked to the sky,
And men stooped down and blessed the beauty rare
That bloomed unconsciously, and served God so.
From peak and glen, from stream and sky went forth
The tokens of the full and glad discharge
Of duty, voiced in all but human speech.

And I—what have I done? My day is blank
Where might been such record down the page
As saints would love to copy; I've no prayer
For blessing on my patient, soulful work.
I hid my talent in the guise of care,
And dreamed away the morn's propitious hours.
I longed to link my name with some pure deed
Done for the love of it and praise to God,
But sat, nor stirred when privilege slipped by.

I brought myself at length to drive a task
I sometimes loved, but had not leisure for.
It ran before me lightly for a while,
But mocked me presently; my heavy hands
Refused to capture it at once, and then
Impatiently I dropped the chase, and turned
To seek in painted streams or window-views
The inspiration for some effort new.

So wore the moments on; and as I crossed
The bridge of noon, and saw men hurry by,
Branded with toil, to taste toil's welcome meed,
A wave of conscience smote me for my fault.

At last the long day died; and with the sun
Went down my jeweled opportunities
Never to rise.   How dim this twilight seems!
The pure, pale moon, now stirring from her couch,
Mist-robed, and girt with sympathetic stars,
Silently shames me, as her nightly beat
She cheerfully begins; there is no note
Of me, most useless usurer of gifts!

Ah, is there no redemption for this loss?
Down from the belfry of eternity
Rings the decree: "Time lost is lost for aye;
But men may mold the remnant of their days
Into mosaics of such divine hue
As shall be built upon the walls of heaven."

Gather around, ye fragments of my life,
That henceforth I may weave, and build, and grave
Statues of nobleness, and garbs of love,
To set in some shy corner of the sky,
And let me sit there, blest if only there.

CONFESSION.

DEAR Christ, Thy blessed name
    Has been my stay,
Thy love to me the same
    For many a day;
But O, my fitful heart
    Has gone astray;
To-night, with many a smart,
    It seeks to pray.

The day's been wondrous fair,
    A story-book,—
A picture of Thy care
    For this earth-nook;
My soul received the gift
    With ill-bred mien;
Thy mercies did not sift
    My faith between.

Thy courts I've been among
    With those who sing;
Thy praise was on my tongue,—
    Lip-offering;
Before Thy shrine I knelt
    To seek Thy face;
My barren breath, I felt
    Defiled the place.

O, Christ, my heart deplores
    Its emptiness!
Ope thou its rusty doors,
    And with faith bless!
If thou my sin canst blot,
    Deign swift reply;
With peace forget me not
    To satisfy!

ON THE SLOPE OF PARNASSUS.

HERE is a height. These trees are cool,
　　These rocks a glorious platform make;
This air is young, and brings back strength
　　Lost in the climb thro' tangled brake.

How steep this path adown the slope!
　　How like a thread it skirts the hill!
And that low meadow,—how content
　　It lies beside that sunny rill!

Those sun-browned rustics, born to toil,
　　Seen listless grown with poor men's fare;
They pl , and reap, and rock their babes,
　　And s are their couch with haggard care.

But *that's* no matter; that dim view
　　Fades from life's background when the eye
Looks swift along the upward slant
　　Of graded honors toward the sky.

Ah, this is life! to feel your height
　　Above the old, dull days that seem
The heritage of want. Come, soul,
　　And weave us now a long, bright dream.

＊　　＊　　＊　　＊　　＊　　＊

But what is all this glory worth ?
　　The past that grew to famous now
Runs on to greatness till a world
　　Pays homage to our laureled brow.

And then ? We die!—How large a sphere
　　Our splendid actions seem to fill!
But in God's universal eye
　　How tame our deeds, our thoughts how ill!

Then here's a world, all full of souls
　　Like ours, with hopes and loves the same;
If their warm tide of loving help
　　Should ebb, what were our icy fame?

Ah, God, how shallow runs our life!
　　Make deep the fount with crystal showers
Of sympathy, that we may bring
　　To Thee a sheaf of grateful flowers.

CHANGELESS.

A DAY of joy and sun and snowdrift spray
　　I paint upon the future; trembling airs
　　Hang o'er the canvas; conscious rapture shares
With questioning my chambered soul; each lay
Of lark or wood thrush tells but of that day,
　　Yet—will it come, the sum of answered prayers?
　　Can mortal break the rosary Time bears?
Or slip of suns in endless circuit stay?
Ah, surer than the pledge of dearest friends,
　　Or love of mother in a sweet child pent,
　　Are God's round years; nor hills nor sounding sea
May bosoms clasp till He shall choose; the ends
　　Of earth swing to His fiat; planned and sent
　　My summer day is, and 'twill come to me.

50

THE GUEST.

THE feast is spread; in solemn state,
In cup and salver consecrate,
The dear gifts asked in prayer await,—
    The broken bread,
    And wine blood-red.

I asked the Lord to sit with me,
To let me all those tokens see,
The marks wrought on the blood-stained tree,
    Of love the sum.
    And will he come?

A step sounds lightly; he is near!
Room for my soul's companion dear,
Blessed the hour that brings him here!
    I scarce can eat,
    His word's so sweet.

He tells me of that anguished night,
Scene of the scourge, the prayer, the flight,
Prelude to Calvary's awesome sight,
    The lifting up,
    The bitter cup.

He shows his tender, gift-used hands,
His feet, his side, with mortal brands,
A ransom offering for all lands,
    O blessed Christ,
    So sacrificed!

I listen to the story low;
My love burns with a clearer glow;
He smiles, and bids me strengthened go.
    I leave his feet
    For use more meet.

MY NEW NAME.

IN vision I part the curtain
   Star-spangled and spun with mist,
Whose drapery blue and crimson
   Earth's last loyal sun has kissed;
I catch from the upper convex
   A shaft of a far sweet light;
And up on the milky ladder
   I climb to its centered height.

The splendor is falling o'er me,
   As pausing with timid feet
I gaze through the jasper doorway,
   And up the long, burnished street.
I wonder if He will know me?
   And whether He'll ask me in ?
I tremble, and wait, and listen,
   And doubts in my faint soul spin!

"My servant that overcometh"—
   The promise I've often read—
"I give as a friendship token
   A precious white stone," it said;
"And deep on its face engraven
   A beautiful name and new,
And sweet with a secret meaning,
   Spelled out with affection true."

O, what will He write on *my* stone?
   "Faith," "Charity," "Joy," or "Trust"?
Or "Patience," or "Loving kindness,"
   Or "Peacemaker," or "The Just"?
I wait still—how long one minute!—
   Perhaps I am not enrolled!
And nameless I'll haunt the portal,
   And sit in its shadows cold!

In terror to earth I'm falling;
    I wake, and I'm sitting here,
But after me calls my Master
    With comforting voice and clear;
"The name I shall keep for you, dear,
    When here at the throne you bow,
Will be but the fitting sequel
    To that you are bearing now."

KEEPING STEP.

'TWAS like a June morn every day;
    As light as swallows' skim
I trod the daisy-sprinkled turf,
    And joined each gladsome hymn;
The sun broke in a thousand gems
    Over the dewy sod;
Most comfortable was my state,
    Because I walked with God.

A dreary drizzling blurred my sky,
    The dripping birds were mute;
A soughing wind swept down the slopes
    And drowned my timid lute;
My neighbors seemed ill in accord;
    Whence such a dismal noon?
My feet were out of step with Him,
    My warped heart out of tune!

53

A VISION.

I'M tired of this new-fashioned life!
   The town's too close and stiff;
Across the blackened chimney-tops
   I watch a sailing cliff;
As virgin snow its beetling brow
   Upon a blue, blue air;
The floating dream comes to my soul
   And stirs a memory there.

Once, when the days were long and blue,
   And honors less than dreams,
I roved the hills unbonneted,
   And waded in the streams;
The shrubby brook thro' meadows ran
   Below the hilly lane
Where summer eves I scrambled up
   Behind the slow-hoofed train.

But O, the orchard was the spot
   In blush-ripe apple-time!
Such cheeks and flavors ne'er were since,
   Save in some poet's rhyme;
But then there were so many trees;
   And I, most human child,
Amidst the sum of present gifts
   Recked not that heaven smiled.

What would I give for one sweet day
   Among the clover heads,
In glad abandon toss me down
   And taste the golds and reds
That swung among the dark green boughs
   With blue sky laughing through,
To pluck of all the trees at will,
   With nothing else to do!

THE UNDISCOVERED.

WHAT lies beyond? Why hangs this veil
    Between to-day and all our dreams?
The past weaves but a prosy tale,
    And mocks at what the future seems.

We sit, and think, and gaze at naught;
    Is life a treadmill? Is our lot
With dull, same fingering to be wrought,—
    A worn-out hope of what is not?

How satisfied our hearts would be
    If Time's slow hand would briefly lift
The vexing curtain! Then could we
    Be free to grasp the future's gift.

And were it fair or dreaded, still
    Would we its utmost meaning know?
Ah, here must halt our errant will;—
    We want its joys; its griefs may go.

Here's our defect of reason; were
    The veil withdrawn and we looked on
Thro' aisles of pain, would we prefer
    A future glimpse to toil that's gone?

We need the lesson of the veil;
    We handle life with too much right;
Our foolish hopes oft kindly fail;
    'Tis calm, sweet trust makes all days bright.

GOD'S PHONOGRAPH.

FINE-WROUGHT and true, the marvelous instrument
Beside the throne of grace and glory stands.
All sounds of human conduct it records,
Gathering songs and wails and hopes and hates
Out of the souls of men so subtly strung,
And tells them out before the angels' court,
Touching the great heart of the holy Lord.
'Tis not the worship of concordant throngs,
With jubilant swell of hallelujah psalm,
To which he soonest listens; there are notes
Of single life that press their simple sound
Upon that faithful chronicle, that catch
His promptest ear; but whether bright and sweet,
Or coarse and sullen, how he smiles or grieves!

One told me that my life was ringing through
That phonograph, and what I said and did
And thought, was echoed in God's very face.
And there, they say, the recording angel sits,
Who copies, word for word, the history
We heedless dictate.   What a power is ours,
By constant chime of gracious words and deeds,
To brighten e'en the effulgence of God's heaven!
Or throw a shade upon that beautiful brow
By playing with the stops of pleasant sins!

So then it is not God, nor his own scribe
That writes our book, for last day witness meant.
We treat the theme ourselves; and O, to think
What wretched stuff we wantonly permit
To be among th' eternal archives stored!
O, soul of mine, look at thy crowded page;
Why hast thou let such unclean things go in ?
For aye repeating and repeating o'er
Exact and full, the instrument speaks on.

When will its utterance be so purified
That it shall chord with every golden harp
That never knew a note save hearty praise!

IN SHADOW.

I 'M weary now; the sun's gone down,
  And twilight blurs my window-pane;
The skirts of night trail o'er the town,
  And wrap my soul with nameless pain.

How happy was I yesterday!
  The sun of love illumined me
And burnished hope, and whispered, "May
  Shall ever scatter blooms for thee!"

But now 'tis dark, and I, alone,
  In labyrinths of doubt am lost;
Could love have led me, had I known
  These lurking phantoms were the cost?

O, heart! thou'rt sadly moved to-night;
  Thy faithlessness deepens the gloom;
Bow to the promise of the light
  And for a richer day make room!

I think, perhaps, if he I love
  Should meet me with the morrow's sun,
And help me look the mists above,
  'Twere easier said, "Thy will be done."

IN AUDIENCE.

IN my little room alone,
   Windows hung with night-shades sable,
On the walls my lamp-gleams thrown,
   Lute and psalter on my table,
Kneeling by my low white bed,
   To a palace I'm translated;
At some throne I droop my head,
   And the air with light is freighted.

Who is this whose voice breaks forth
   Gently as the zephyrs vernal,
Chasing black clouds to the north,
   Throbbing with a note supernal?
Who am I that grasp the feet
   Bound with sandals gemmed with glory?
(At the deed my pulses beat)
   Never ventured bard such story.

'Tis my King! and I have dared
   Thus to come at His inviting;
Strange his majesty has cared
   Thus to hear my soul's inditing;
For this council-chamber rang
   With the eloquence of sages;
Princes, seers and poets sang
   Anthems here for long, dim ages.

Am I dreaming? Is this true,
   That the Patron of earth's gifted,—
David, who himself o'erthrew,
   Moses, strong, with hand uplifted,
Paul, evangel of the dawn,—
   Stoops to catch *my* trembling phrases,
Touches me to urge me on,
   On my bowed head sweetly gazes?

'Tis a thrilling, marvelous truth!
  There's no higher crown or station
Than God's dowried love and ruth,—
  This His blessedest oblation.
Clad in purples or in alms,
  Here all souls are of one measure;
For all woes are boundless balms,
  For all need an endless treasure.

GULFS.

THERE is no perfect union; friends may swear
  Eternal fellowship, and vow to die
  Each for the other; heart-beat may reply
To heart-beat, and the fervent lovers share
Supremest weal and hope, or woe and care,
  Yet separate fears and longings that defy
  All bridging, make the dearest mortal tie
A simple clasping hands of twin-born prayer.
The Framer of the heart alone hath sight
  And feeling for our various human moods;
He floods each thought with strong, assuring light,
  And on our secret dream His knowledge broods;
From Him nor life nor death can us divide,
With His communion we are satisfied.

UNREST.

I SCARCELY know
If I have cause for joy or gloom.
My heart, alone within my room,
With longing beats, yet feels the bloom
    On glad cheeks glow.

    Is this my fate,
O Father? Warm's the life I've met;
Thou offerest refuge from the fret
And toil of work-day life, and yet—
    Is it my fate?

    O, I have prayed
That I might clasp Thy guiding hand,
That on Faith's ladder I might stand
And know what good, through Thy command,
    For me has stayed.

    My doubting soul
Fears to accept Thy tendered boon;
For me of joy some brighter noon
May wait; must I give up so soon
    This sweeter goal?

    It seems so fair;
Yes, Father, I have thought it best;
Some deep, full joy may fill my breast
And give my heart the truer rest,—
    So sweet and rare.

    Peace is hard won;
Dost Thou know best? O, pity me!
Make me content Thy hand to see,
And lose myself in that grand plea,
    "Thy will be done."

MY SPHERE.

A LITTLE round of duties, hopes and cares
That jar sometimes and spoil the perfect poise
Of life which God hath meted; longing shares
With glad reflection past and future joys,
But still the scale's uneven; never pride
Of old attainment at some petty theme
Can balance what I wait for in the wide,
Rich Possible, my purpose and my dream.

Is it not right that I should strive to break
The close-knit limits of this small, dull orb
Which my best flights but commonplaces make,
While threadbare deeds my precious time absorb?
Sure, it were grander to be lord than slave,
And wiser to have plenty than be poor;
'Twere nobler, too, to front the world with brave
And high-souled zeal than grope in haunt obscure.

Ah, what is this? A strong wind rushes by
My rocky cleft, and after it a voice
So small, so deep, it seems a summer sigh,
Breaks up the calm expectance of my choice.
It glorifies my narrow house, and turns
The sober gray of duty into gold;
The lonely light of simple living burns
With fresh-trimmed splendor in its setting old.

It cheers me so, I care not now for room
To walk the wider range of ampler spheres;
I am content to see a daisy bloom,
And know that everywhere God's hand appears;
I shall be grateful to His liberal will
If I can only tend one little spot,
And both my hands with humble blossoms fill,
And make them say to Him, "Forget me not."

IV.

THE UPLANDS.

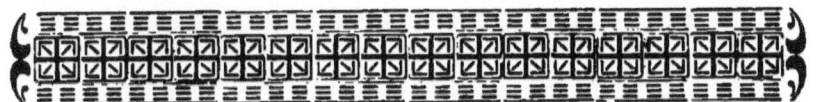

A PRISON SONG.

NOT skylark's transport, in the blue, faint deep
　　Where bird and sun, lone summer comrades, **play,**
　　Nor nightingale, whose mellow madrigal
The moonless wood to dreamy echo stirs,
Nor caged thing, with full, impassioned throat
Pouring its hymn into the work-day world,
A finer essence of earth's melody
Into the exquisite ear of heaven distils
Than that brave jubilate in the cell
Of clammy Philippi, where two strong souls
Fluttered, mindless of rudely fettered feet,
Startling the dead of night to sudden song
That through the rusty grates went billowing
Till all the prisoners heard.
　　　　　　　　　　Sublime content,
That 'mid the clouds a-wing, or clipped and bound,
No note effaces from its gamut clear
Of heartful praise to God beneficent,
Who turns all happenings to glorious good!

ASPIRATION.

O FOR the hills of green,
Crowned with a summer sheen,
   That kiss the sky;
Where angel wings are heard
Whose flights the planet gird,
Where shady airs are stirred
   With melody.

God walks in gardens there
With sainted souls and rare,
   Heroes in deed;
O, for the peace that thrills
When comradeship so fills
The heart, and rich Love wills
   Gift for all need.

Afar the summits gleam
Like structures of a dream,
   Thrones of the just;
My feet are wet with clay,
To gather weeds I stay;
When dies the patient day
   They turn to dust.

O, heights that great hearts find,
I cast this life behind,
   And call to you;
In "heavenly places" sweet
Be't mine those hearts to greet,
And kiss the Master's feet
   A creature new.

LISTENING FOR THE BELLS OF ETERNITY.

WHEN the morn is smiling on the summer world,
　　And the spring of music hides in every tree,
　　While the quiet sunbeams wander thro' the blue,
And the forest river murmurs to the sea,
As we dream and wonder, all the shapes of song
　Mingle in one cadence from the world to be;
And the message thrills us, and we wait and pray,
　Listening for the bells of eternity.

When the blazing noontide walks the ripening fields,
　And the wild bee's droning fills the sultry hours,
When the stony highway bruises weary feet,
　And the dust has blighted all the gladsome flowers,
Sheaf by sheaf we gather, with a toil-worn hand,
　Fainting for a zephyr from the cooling sea;
But we're hushed a moment, and our hearts look up,
　Listening for the bells of eternity.

When the peaceful sunset pours its softened gold
　O'er the chastened furrows, and the toilers true,
Faintly from the village peal the vesper bells,
　Like a breath from heaven　born of fresh'ning dew;
Reverently we hearken; as the last note dies
　Into solemn silence o'er the daisied lea,
In a surge of rapture to the stars we turn,
　Listening for the bells of eternity.

TARRYING BY THE STUFF.

'MID hail of lead, and smoke of bombs,
   Pelting the army's front,
Brave souls, for right and honor's sake,
   Shoulder the battle's brunt;
O'er fallen hosts the dear flag floats,
   And to the cheerful drum,
Each man a hero, powder-burnt,
   The troops come marching home.

Waiting for news, the frailer ones,
   Patient, though prest with care,
Fill up the long days in far homes
   Watching the altars there;
Keeping the children and the sick,
   Knitting and mending gowns,
Eating and sleeping in the hills,
   And in the lonely towns.

With trophy-laden companies
   The hamlets are alive,
And plumes and breast-marks nod and flare
   When the last troops arrive;
How shall the hard-earned spoil be shared
   'Twixt these, who brought it in,
And these, who kept the household stuff
   Far from the martial din?

How equitable the decree—
   As one, so the other's part!
Comfort your souls, ye least of His,
   And blind and halt, take heart!
All cannot pluck fame's amaranth,
   Some must be kitchen queens;
Yet for best service anywhere—
   Life and a crown it means!

UPWARD.

DUSK slowly falls upon the day of rest;
   The old-time quiet fills the air in-doors;
   With separate meditation throbs each breast,
  And now and then a thought to heaven soars.
A face beside the window seeks for light,
  Not of the day, but for a yearning soul
Hungry for full communion, never quite
  Attained to, with the One to whom the whole
Creation looks in fervent gratitude.
  The outlook bars the door to passing prayer;
A wintry street wraps thought in cheerless mood;
  The town's so full of houses; here and there
A human figure glides among them; roofs,
  Some black with age, some new, their patch-work flaunt
Toward the sky; the snow patched hills are proofs
  Of strong environment; the sere woods daunt
The searching gaze, the restless wish for peace.
  But just outside the window stands a tree;
In fresh endeavor for the earth's release
  The eye now scales the black, stiff boughs, all free
Of bloom or leaf, unto the topmost branch,
  And catching its mute pointing, leaps away
From sense into the blank, gray ether, stanch
  And vast, where nothing is, save dying day.

Ah, there is God! He fills the spaces where
  Earth cannot touch, nor e'er is reached by man,
Save as he lifts himself, engirt by prayer,
  And steers straight up to Him whose fingers span
The planets, nor too mighty are to hold
  The little life of creatures, and whose ears
The music of a praiseful breath enfold,
  Counting it rarer than the chime of spheres.

LIFE–MUSIC.

A CROSS from my busy window,
  In the glare of the afternoon,
Besides a shadeless chimney,
  Intent with a strong, fresh tune,
A robin perched and caroled,
  All glad in a solar sea,
And a livelong hour kept singing,
  I thought, to comfort me.

And then I worked the harder
  In the strength that music gave,
And I thanked the bird in secret
  For his wild, sweet song so brave;
And then he flew elsewhither,
  Some other heart to bless
Which pined in thankless toiling
  For nature's least caress.

Late in the summer gloaming,
  At work by my lamplight's glare,
The few, faint notes of an organ
  I heard, embalmed in the air;
My quick soul caught at the echo,
  Rehearsed it to my pen;
So I write that men may listen
  For music in life's dark glen.

Say, why should our life be dismal?
  Our cares are full of song,
Our sadness set in rainbows,
  Our weary arms are strong,
When a bird, or brook, or zephyr
  Absorbs our kindling sense;
The sultry air grows fresher,
  With laughing fairies dense.

With never a thought for the morrow,
    Singing the time away,
The choirs of nature greet us
    To chide our sad-faced day.
Why, with our mighty reason,
    Should we, with smaller trust
Than a wee, red-throated robin,
    Thinks ours a lot less just?

REINFORCEMENT.

(2 Kings 6: 17.)

O SOJOURNER in Dothan, art afraid
    Because the walls are pelted by the foe,
    Seeking thy peaceful dwelling's overthrow,
And none stands forth to give thee friendly aid?

Dost shrink because a giant stalking sin
    Creeps round thy roof and shakes the timbers loose,
    Batters thy heart and takes for baser use
Thy loves and hopes, and all thou trustedst in?

Open thine eyes, O servant of the King!
    Thou art not left alone in strife so dire;
    Behold the chariots and steeds of fire
Sweeping the hills around from wing to wing.

Never to self is left the one who dares
    Battle for right, or hearth and land defend;
    Stronger is he with only God as friend,
Than legions else, tho' all applause be theirs.

CO-WORKERS.

SUCH a wondrous task to do!
Skies to paint with brush of blue,
Worlds to hang their depths amid,
Wheel and orbits swift to bid;
Sun to make for planet dear,
Snow and leaf from year to year;
Fields to kiss to fruitage rare,
Lakes to smooth for mirrors fair.

Greater far than deeds in stone,
Sea, or air with star-blooms sown,
Is the work in human souls,
Which one Artisan controls;
Seeds of love and truth to sow,
Hearts to watch that they may grow;
Arrowed words to strike at sin,
Gilded vice to virtue win.

Such a marvelous work, meseems,
Were desire of angels' dreams;
Yet our God has made decree
That His helpers *we* should be;
In the busy ranks to stand,
Here, or there, at his command;
Sweetening days for those who toil,
Guarding innocence from soil.

O, such privilege divine!
That our hands may intertwine
God's strong hand, and labor so
For the glad millennium's glow!
Keep us, Father, stanch and true,
Faith in Thy sure Word renew;
In Thy smile we fear no storm,
In Thy name our deeds perform.

YOKE-FELLOWS.

I USED to worry at a new-set task,
Or large responsibility of life,
Fearing the load and I unequal; nights
I dreamed of weird solutions, or sublime
Finales; but my parting eyelids flashed
The photograph of yestern harassment,
And slow, unrested, I arose to meet
The gray daybreak, and slipped my work-gear on.
And so my time and toil went dragging; chafed
With present frets, and scarred from past missteps,
And fearful of to-morrow's outcome, least
I deemed me 'mong the stalwarts in the faith.

One songful morrow, when somehow the rose
And emerald of earth and sky half crazed
The larks, and me distraught a reverent space,
A light hand touched me; turning, at my side
I saw my Elder Brother yoked with me,
Straining with more than half the load. He smiled:
" 'Tis not so heavy now, is it, my friend?"
How blind I was! such service to ignore!
My Lord my servant!   Always more than friend,
He begs the larger share of all our woes,
Content if we but keep abreast with Him.
Greater commission I have since received;
But now I know that noblest images
Ourselves may rear, and find it sweet employ,
Thro' Him whose hand directs the chiseling.

73

WHEELS.

STOOD forth from his masterful fingers
　An artisan's wondrous design;—
A myriad wheels ran their circles,
　Obedient to subtile combine;
Some swift, with the hum of the busy,
　Some slow, like the great mill-wheel's drone;
Some giants, and some small as dew-drops;
　Some crosswise—but none wrought alone.

The artisan, tenderly gazing
　On the beautiful child of his thought,
Soon noticed a rough sound of discord,
　And anxious the culprit he sought;
A small wheel, for envy of larger,
　A quiet one, fretting at noise,
A great one, disturbed by the cross-wheels,
　Had stopped, in rebellious poise.

　　*　　*　　*　　*　　*　　*

O, world! does the parable touch you?
　Humanity's made of such wheels;
Some heroes are known the world over;
　A "shut in" no clarion peals;
There are who must gather the harvests,
　And those who the mysteries teach;
While "least ones" are set among gardens,
　And martyrs beatitude reach.

O, spoilers of God's good creation!
　When, loth to revolve in your sphere,
You long for a large place to dwell in,
　And chafe at the cross-winds so drear;
Know fully the plan of the Maker:
　Each soul shall *his own* work fulfill,
And wrapped in a trusting contentment,
　Lie down under guard of His will.

A SUBLIME BATTLE.

THE gilded citadel of sin
　With turrets, domes, and pennons gay,
Looks the pure, broad sun in the eye
　Unblushing 'neath his tell-tale ray;
The ramparts bristle with keen arms,
　Hedging each new crime's birth;
Who shall destroy this Jericho,
　The plague of God's clean earth?

Up the bald cliff a handful stout,
　By pledge of reinforcement spurred,
Sans sword or shield, with faith superb,
　Presses in rank, without a word;
No more absurd could be their arms—
　A ram's rude wrinkled horn—
Whereat the watchmen stop to play,
　And laugh to heaven their scorn.

Day after day, with measured tramp,
　Circle the mocking citadel
The silent buglers; the dull sound
　Smites on the ear like some far knell;—
A sudden blast shivers the air,
　A grand shout rends the walls,
And o'er the leprous brood of sin
　The crack of doomsday falls!

No matter, friend, what granite towers
　Shelter the deeds of Belial's sons,
Or how their blustering regiments
　Level at right their impious guns,
Before the echoing blast of truth,
　With God's wings closing round,
Their mightiest stronghold shall be razed,
　Its ashes sow the ground!

THE MAIDEN'S PRAYER.

LOW she knelt where rose-hued curtains
　　Flung soft color o'er the room;
Knelt beside her open casement,
　　On her face devotion's bloom.
Not adown the bordered gravel,
　　Where the moon played on the grass,
Nor the elms' long cloistered shadows
　　Did her reverent vision pass.

But beyond the silver twinkle
　　Of the first-born evening star,—
Tiny rift of heavenly glory,—
　　Sped her heart and gaze afar.
Lips of praise essayed to follow,
　　Framed in heavy, mortal phrase,
Breaking into fervent pleading
　　For redemption of her days:—

"Father holy!　King majestic!
　　If from out the jeweled sky
Thy pure eyes can find this altar,
　　Let them rest ere passing by!
All my soul looks for thy coming
　　With a trembling, loving awe;
For I must my heart unburden
　　Of its weight of broken law.

"O, how large has been Thy dealing
　　Of dear health and daytime joy!
And Thy tireless arms, O Maker,
　　All the harms of night destroy.
Yet how much has grown my talent?
　　What new light have I diffused?
O, abide! rare wealth of mercy,
　　That so hardly I have used.

"Let my wilful tongue and fingers
　　Find resource from purer life;
Press high thoughts, O God, upon me,
　　With Thy love and beauty rife.
Make my feet to run glad errands,
　　Bearing gifts to sorrow's door;
Consecrate my lightest heart-throbs
　　To Thy glory evermore!"

Then there fell a wondrous rustling
　　On her soul's attentive ear;
Out o'er heaven's border bending
　　Angels smiled her words to hear.
Round the Throne then bowed the harpers,
　　Breathed the maiden's prayer again;
God his swift response sent earthward,
　　Answered with a sweet "Amen!"

A DREAM OF MANHOOD.

HE must be great; but whether tall or fair
　　It matters not; the stature of his soul
　　Shall dignify his body, and enroll
His heart with sacred things, so pure and rare
With liquid love that one clear beam from air
　　Celestial will to rainbows turn the whole
　　Of his sweet earth-life, and his thought control
To pity, help, forgive, believe, forbear.
He must be true; no gilt words shall beguile
　　His lip to trifle, nor his face to lie;
　　　With tender grace his hand shall scatter balm
On wounded friendship, and restore the smile
　　To care-old orphans.　So he shall not die,
　　　But shine, star-crowned, in Heaven's bluest
　　　　calm.

THE CLOUD.

I RAISED my eyes to westward
  As twilight softly fell;
I leaned against the window,
  Drawn by a dreamy spell;
The sky was amber-tinted,
  Clear as a glassy sea,
Save where one somber cloudlet
  The splendor marred for me.

I watched it sail,—it drew me,
  It looked so boldly dark,—
When, as I gazed intently,
  It lost its primal mark;
The outlines broke and softened
  And seemed to melt away,
And lo! to my strained vision
  All cloudless closed the day.

Thus, in life's latest prospect,
  I thought, how grand twill be
To find our clouds and shadows
  Beyond the sunset flee;
When every one who suffered
  And prayed and trusted long,
Will find his sky at evening
  All light, and peace, and song.

Ah, soul, know now the Master;
  His ways are not like ours;
For whom He loves He chastens,—
  He breaks the choicest flowers.
O, if this grief, this burden,
  Is proof of love divine,
Then rest, my soul, and whisper,
  "Not my desire, but Thine!"

THE CHAMBER ON THE WALL.

(2 Kings 4: 10.)

TURN in, O man of God, awhile;
   See, we have built this nook for rest,
A goal for many a sandaled mile,
   A home for thee, our welome guest.

Make it thine own; here read and pray;
   Solace thy limbs upon this bed;
Let thy good presence with us stay,
   And with us break our evening bread.

     *   *   *   *   *

O, Son of God, thou traveler worn,
   Come to my chambered heart to-night;
Thy skirts and hands with briers are torn
   Thy locks with Hermon dews bedight.

I long for thy sweet company,
   And press thee to my humble board;
Eat of my store—'tis served for thee,
   And 'neath my roof be thou restored.

CABLES.

THERE is a heart-home somewhere in the deep,
  Star-misty concave, fashioned of a Thought,
  With gem-set doors and light-spun curtains
      wrought,
Where rhythmic waters under green banks sweep,
Where skies their faultless balm and tintings keep,
  And sweet-faced neighbors think and speak of naught
  But pure-white truth and loving-kindness, caught
In that blest air, which needs no charm of sleep.
'Tis *our* home, *my* home! built and kept for me,
  By my best Friend. I may not go there yet;
  But every day I send a message up,
And ask; "Art there?" Word flashes back—'tis He!
So trust I; and this waiting I'll forget
  When I shall drink from His own vintage cup.

IN TRANSIT.

THE swift aphelion of his life's ellipse
  A soul is crossing, out of thought eterne
  Projected, lit with energies that burn
Their influence on beholders; lightly slips
His rosary of years; through chance eclipse
  His graciousness and truth more brightness earn;
  Aye to his orbit's axle his eyes turn,
Lode-star toward which his noble impulse dips.
But now the interplanetary chill
  Strikes him; his head is sown with delicate frost,
    His round limbs shrink, his gait majestic slows,
Yet patiently the home-track keeps until,
  All weight of weariness in lethe lost,
    Clasped to the heart of God he finds repose.

THRONES.

WHAT shall we do in God's supernal courts?
Befriended by his princely Son, who gave
Most generous titles and estates, we're told
That shimmering thrones are standing near God's own,
Waiting, with power to rule, our entrance there.
But we, who go about in mortal life
Finding our work where holier feet once went
Bearing the comfortable words of hope,
Substantial alms, and doctrines full of faith,
And service free, and self-abasement,—why,
When all our joy is in this blessed cause,
And *brotherhood* brings up the noblest souls,
Should we aspire to dignities unused
And illy fitting our plebeian rank,
To sit as princes, and to give commands?

For me I beg a shady garden nook
Where I may watch the ripples in the stream
That carries life about all heaven, and pluck
A Sharon rose to wear upon my breast,
With joy o'erbrimming in that perfect spring.
The palaces upon the hills may gleam,
And royal companies may throng the halls;
If only I'm inside the jasper wall,
A simple robe that God shall give me then,
A voice to sing his praise, and liberty
To walk with him and Christ among the trees,
Will fill the highest dreamings of my soul.

'HOW are they gettin' along?" says the good-wife,
    a-pouring the tea;
    For "father" has brought from the village a letter
    from far Tennessee;
And rubbing his time-honored spectacles he plants them
    astride of his nose,
And reading the badly-spelled message a gleam o'er his
    grizzled face glows.

"Deer father an' mother," it ran, "I hope you are hearty
    an' well;
We're gettin' along first-rate, tho' Jimmy was sick a
    spell;
Our crops have turned out middlin', but of apples we'll
    have a heap;
An' out in the back lot pastur's a peart little flock o'
    sheep.

"We've plenty o' good milk an' butter, and everything
    needful to eat;
But something we've got better yet, an' we call it just
    "darlin'" an' "sweet";
Her eyes an' her hair are like coal, an' she's smilin' an'
    chipper an' strong,
So savin' a wee bit more workin', I think we are gettin'
    along."

    *   *   *   *   *   *

We're "getting along," and whither? some path we are
    leaving behind
As foot after foot we measure and over the uplands we
    wind;
Are skies growing rarer, and brooklets more clear as we
    press farther on?
Are new fields and harvests more winsome as old times
    and landscapes are gone?

We're "getting along,"—how speed we? Past mile-stones
    of honor and truth?
Through valleys illumined with virtue, the great-
    hearted champion of youth?
Up hillsides where charities flourish, of service the ever-
    green crown?
'Mid city-smoked rafters and spirits, where love brings
    our only renown?

Yes, thus leads the road to the kingdom, the goal of all
    "getting" and toil;
In passing through brambles and byways our garments
    and hands suffer soil;
But thanks to the foreseeing Builder, our pathway can
    never go wrong,
And he who treads closest its turnings, is surest of "get-
    ting along."

THE INEXHAUSTIBLE.

A MAN, in airs of courts sublime arrayed,
    Mercy and majesty in deep eyes blent,
    Over the hard, hot road on errand went
To stay the passing breath of some sweet maid.
Among the throng that pressed him, half afraid
    One strained to touch his trailing hem; she meant
    To draw sure healing unawares; attent
To that swift thrill, his course he stayed.
"Who touched me?" Ah, my Lord and Healer true,
    I needed thee so much, and thou art great,
    Full as the sea thy store, which grows not less
By liberal gifts to cloud and lake, whose due
    They pour back in its bosom; nor abate
    Thou of thy grace the suffering world to bless.

THE CHILD'S GATE.

THERE is a rosy suburb
  This way from Paradise,
Where bells of laughter tinkle,
  Where sparkle dew-bright eyes;
Where innocence and beauty
  Grow on the self-same stem,
And trust, with sun-lines written,
  Glows like a new-cut gem.

Here in their fragrant cradles
  The round, sweet babies lie
While heads with nodding ringlets
  To blithe-voiced birds reply;
The touch of angel florists
  Keeps fresh this border-land,
Blushing with morn's caresses,
  By upper zephyrs fanned.

Piercing the green wall midway
  A tall gate busily swings,
Through which the curious children
  Catch sight of wondrous things;
Man's wide estates stretch boundless,
  And from a hundred towers
That touch the eagle's level
  His eye the blue rim scours.

The busy gate swings faster;
  With sudden eagerness
The dazzled little playmates
  Into the grown world press;
They scatter without farewell,
  They drift to every zone,
Seeking, by this or that path,
  Some Lookout Peak, their own!

At cost of daily drudging,
  Out from the thinning crowds
A few are high on ladders
  That lean against the clouds;
The winds of care are blowing;
  The frosty film of doubt
Creeps o'er their tender child hearts,
  And kills love's rootlets out.

In books and business delving,
  In court, in field, in mine,
They've lit the lamp of reason,
  Forgot sweet faith's star-shine;
The Tempter's silk-spun cobwebs
  Grow into ropes of sin;
The voice of truth is stifled
  In this great live world's din.

"For self," the hidden motto;
  "For good," the bolder sign;
While nations rock and crumble
  Which traitors undermine;
And O! the pity of it!
  This world's so far from heaven;—
Its pure endeavors throttled,—
  So close is honor driven!

"None but the humble child-life
  May enter Paradise;"
Swing on, unresting portal,
  Let mortals pass thee twice!
Back in the sun and daisies
  That border youth's sweet vale,
O man, sit down and rest thee,
  These airs divine inhale!

The innocents oft wander
Upon the mystic beach;
To flitting angel-shadows
Their eager arms they reach;
Like them, live glad and trustful,
Just within Love's clear call,
Who yearns over His offspring,
And cries, "I want them all!"

THE DIVINE BOYHOOD.

SUCH a wondrous tale was told me
Of a child in Eastern clime,
Clothed with wondrous gift of wisdom,—
Prodigy of all that time;
At his birth they named him "Jesus,"
Token of his mission blest;
All the world should have a Saviour,
And a Strength, a Song, a Rest.

Fair above all other children,
Winning with his modest ways,
Serious thought his eyes o'erbrimming,
Gentle in his childish plays,
He, his happy mother's idol,
Pondered things she could not know,
Strove to grasp his Father's secret,
Full release from human woe.

Did he, as his fancy led him
Thro' the meadows thick with herds,
Or upon the breezy hillside,
Or in woods in tune with birds,—

Did he think of mass and color,
　Dappled sky and templed hill?
Or upon the human heart-ache
　God-sent love alone could still?

Ah, the thoughts that swelled his bosom!
　E'en his mother, in her joy,
Wondered, as she saw unfolding
　Godlike wisdom in her boy;
Was he thinking of the future,
　Storing strength of mind and soul
For the stress of sin and sorrow?
　Did he see his brief life's goal?

When a dozen golden summers
　On his brow had left their mark,
Foregleams of a mighty manhood,
　Like a sunbeam in the dark,
Flashed upon the temple sages
　Who the holy Scriptures taught;
Saw they now their truer meaning
　By the light this God-child brought.

Thus he grew to noble stature,
　Blessed of God and praised of men,
Learning life's sublimest lessons,
　Teaching others o'er again;
Thus may we, O Son of heaven,
　Lay thy tender life to heart;
Teach us now, by thy dear presence,
　Love's divine and perfect art.

THE LAST ACT.

THE players all save one have left the stage;
As chime the nearby bells with sudden stroke
The final curfew of the year, he starts,
To find the dim lights to their sockets burnt,
And pit and gallery empty; the rough wind
Rattles the windows, and its rasping voice
Wails o'er the open grave where presently
This last short day will sleep beside its kin.

A throng of wingèd whispers flit around,
And swing before his quick, wide-open eyes
Medleys of words, outlined on various ground,
That for the twelvemonth past the fabric wove
Of life and character now brought to test.
"Show me thy way" close-joined with "I know
        best;"
"I give a tithe," "The poor I can't abide;"
"I never steal" and "Drive a bargain close;"
"I mind my own affairs" and "What's the news?"
"Be patient, Lord," and "Such a stupid child!"
"I'm prompt at church," "A prosy sermon that!"
"Fill me with love," "'Tis good enough for him!"
"Come, Christ, again," "I cannot die just yet;"
"Save me from sin," "This life's a pleasant dream!"

Once and again the phantoms round him whirl
And ask him why the sprouts of kindness died
Untimely, and the crust of worldly fame
Sealed up his fleshly heart, and why he failed
To shoulder Truth tho' he stooped to't alone?

And now a mellow light breaks over them,
Its focus on the kneeling actor's head;
The wild wind checks its sob, and in the hush
Two hands are lifted in imploring clasp,

And tears empearl the cheeks; a silvery Voice,
Whose emphasis is *mercy*, thrills his soul.
The phantoms vanish; he's alone with God.

(Curtain falls.)

ROSES.

ALL day the rose I plucked in dew
  And wore with knot of ribbon white,
From dying life sweet fragrance drew,
  Calling my thoughts from vagrant flight
Into the dreamy air of peace,
  And rest in toil, and mountain views
Of azure calms and banks of fleece,
  Strewing the heaven with happy hues.

There are some roses, not of red
  Or creamy petals, nor perfumed
With June's brief odors, whose folds shed
  Their rarest scent when they have bloomed.
Such is true friendship; when its buds
  Open to trust and sympathy,
Its unlocked heart of fragrance floods
  Each giver in a perfumed sea.

But when the shapely, cherished flower
  Sprinkles the turf, and our friend dies,
What mellow memories bless each hour,
  What incense floats to purple skies!
Sever no friend whose faith is true;
  Succor his soul in storm or slight;
Wear roses, fresh with virtue's dew,
  Bound with love's ribbon, pure and white.

V.

APPRENTICESHIP.

APPRENTICESHIP.

THE Master looketh on.   How daintily strung
 Our rosary of deeds!   We sort our tools,
Keen-bright with eager service; set among
 Staunch, hoary oaks, we bide their well-tried rules;
We spread, touch leaf with fellow, gaining some
 Of thoroughness, and giving courage back;
We dole the hungry poor a generous crumb,
 Exhaling smiles where most of joy there's lack;
We walk abroad at noon, and pluck and burn
 The weeds of vice, and bring a sweet, pure dawn;
We serve, and kitchens into rose-beds turn;
 We do all this, the Master looking on.

The Master is invisible.   How rough
 This thread, how gnarled this fiber!   Well, time
   fleets,
Our quota must be done; 'tis good enough.
 We spy an idle chum, and play at cheats;
We daub our canvas, or we drop a stitch;
 We run about to find an easy place.
And leave off burnishing our homely niche,
 Fretting for palms that greet the well-won race.
As thus we slight our serving, and complain,
 Behold a sudden writing on the wall!
Fear-struck, our faithfulness we dare not feign;
 We stand revealed; the Master sees it all!

ROUTINE.

ANOTHER night is ended,
   Another day begun;
Around the same world speedeth
   The same old glowing sun.

The yesterdays are risen
   All ruthless from their tomb,
And rob the young to-morrow
   Of all its hopeful bloom.

The same old tale's repeated
   Of effort and regret,
Of lessons that discourage,
   Of quick fatigue and fret.

The plain is tame and idle,
   The sky is nothing new;
The tree are greenly irksome,
   And every flower is blue.

The tide of morning glory
   Is buried in eclipse;
'Tis but a common chalice
   The Fates press to our lips.

The wheel and whirl of duty
   Joins evening with the dawn;
And while we work and wonder
   Another day is gone.

So suns burn through the zenith,
   And white moons wax and wane;
A page of life's turned over,
   Begun the same worn strain.

Give patient trust, O Father,
    While days go lagging past;
We wait Thy rare exalting
    When time shall breathe its last.

LIFE'S SPIRAL.

LIKE the pink opening of a whorlèd shell
Life opens broad in its initial years.
How far apart the mile-stones of our youth!
Thro' summer, autumn, snow, and loitering spring
The little feet grow tired at the long round.
And while the peachy bloom is on the cheeks
Of charming innocence, how oft the plaint,
"O, mama, how I wish the time would come!"
And by and by it comes; but as the mind
Grows used to things after the first success,
And goals recurring dull the new suspense,
The circles shorten; each new year the whorl
Brings birthdays closer in concentrate course.
And by and by we hear the cry amazed,
"How flies the time!" And still the years close in,
Crowding the duties, cares, desires, and hopes
In smaller compass, till at last they blend
Into a point,—the very top of life.
Blessed the exit, if that summit touch
The sphere of larger and eternal life,
Where light and joy, and peace, and praise revolve
Around the universal center, God!

BETWEEN SHORES.

A MORNING zephyr fans the bay,
A blush o'erspreads the clouds of gray.
Closed moored, a barque with dallying spray
  Is turned about;
With sun-browned cheek and ringlets free,
A boy, in garlands all a-glee,
Looks with mild wonder on the sea;
  The tide is out.

His ears are charmèd with the tone
Of laugh, and dirge, and dying moan,
And hoarse repeatings; all alone,
  His fancies glow;
He hurries boatward thro' the sand,
Grasps its wet side with dimpled hand,
And floats off gaily from the strand:
  The tide is low.

With fresh delight he rocks his barge
The distance shoreward to enlarge;
Sweet skies and waves some charm discharge
  Of fairy spell;
The faintest bird-calls now on shore
Die out; dear landmarks loom no more,
But murmurs now, unheard before,
  The tidal swell.

Dark grows the blue, wide sea; afar
Aurora's steeds a somber car
Roll skyward; winds the vessel jar
  With sob and sigh;
Hard-strained, the barque flies with the gale;
The youth in vain looks for a sail,
And screaming sea-birds turn him pale;
  The tide is high.

The air grows thick and blacker; haste
Live thunders o'er the briny waste;
The rim 'twixt wave and cloud's effaced,
　　　Hope well-nigh gone;
The strong man seeks, with muscle tense,
The outlet to the shadow dense,
And toward his best deeds' consequence
　　　The tide rolls on.

The storm is spent; each scudding cloud
Its haughty exit has allowed;
Ethereal calms the boat enshroud,
　　　No longer tossed;
Before the veteran now appears
A perfect landscape, and he hears
Most homelike voices; die all fears
As on that beach of timeless years
　　　The tide is lost.

"AS A MUSTARD SEED."

FROM a gray clod a tiny shoot upsprings,
　　Stretches its limbs, and blinks in the broad sun;
　　As cheerfully abroad its branches run,
I ask, "What dost thou 'midst these weedy things?"
"My Master me divine provision brings,
　　And bids me grow and bless; how can I shun
　　His will? If I but woo and shelter one
Stray bird, I'm recompensed whene'er it sings."
O faithless! must your hearts be taught so oft
　　By things inglorious to proclaim the light
　　　Of prodigal beneficence to men,
The laboring hands, and eyes that look aloft,
　　The sacrifice in deserts wide and white
　　　Of life itself, expecting not again?

RIPENESS.

OLD gold and purple, brown and red and pale
Leafage and fruit upon the year's full brow
Lie mingled; 'tis a rare and bounteous smile
Lights up October's finely-chiseled face,
Victorious grown thro' storms and summer suns
Which knew not wherefore they were sent; but God,
With sweet design of beauty farther on
And deep, wide joy which never June could bring,
Mysterious errands gave them; and they blew,
And scorched, and drenched the mid-year life, which
    sighed
Anon, and grieved; but now 'tis all forgot
How ill it seemed, and autumn's crimson blush
Bespeaks a heart of glad benevolence.

There is a world of tender human souls
Which scarce have bloomed before a fretting care
Or ill-timed sorrow blots their sunny hours,
And clouds of pain hang wearily o'er the scene
For only joy perennial purposed; storms
Which shake some friendships loose, and drop us out
From honored notice into studied slight,
Begin to rock our faith; some noble plans,
For good designed, are crossed; the likeliest deed
To win warm praise a bitter judgment finds.

We stop our fruitless work, and question God.
Why drifts this haze about us, blurring all
Our charity intended, all the glad,
Sweet joys of life, darkly enveloping
Our spirits, standing like a tree well pruned,
With half its severed limbs upon the ground?
A sudden whirlwind clears away the mist;
Only thro' seeming thankless toil, and long

But patient care, and solemn, chastening griefs,
Which trim our souls to fuller bearing, may
Our faithful eyes behold the Providence
Whose reapers will transplant us to the sky.

STILL WATERS.

MY heart was like a placid lake
    Engirt with sun-clad hills, whose shade
Scarce touched the brim; but half awake
    The summer wind upon it played.

A sudden squall from out the west
    Its bosom struck; the quick waves rose
Rebellious from their troubled rest,
    And flood met flood as uttered foes.

The tempest stirred the deep sea sand;
    Then, lashed and weary, moaned the lake
For peace; and lo! a spirit's hand
    Stilled all, nor let a ripple break.

So works the Master with the heart;
    When life is summery, and the soul
With warm friends dwells, with mystic art
    He tries our faith and turns our goal.

Resentment greets the offered change;
    It holds not our ideal fate;
We darkly pass the trial strange
    And wonder why light comes so late.

We will not see the hidden love
    Which schools our trust and rights our will;
Till, spent with strife, we look above:
    Swift comes in answer, "Peace, be still!"

IN THE MILL.

"LORD, make me pure!" the strong plea throneward
   flies;
  Thereat God sets in motion all the wheels,
 And we are crushed and broken, as He deals
The stroke bereaving, and our rain-wet eyes
Strain upward thro' the mist; the Hand replies
 With grief's full baptism to our low appeals
 For cleansing, till our sifted spirit kneels
Among the sinless hosts of Paradise.
"Lord, make me pure!" Ah, know we what we ask?
  Like wheat which fain would be a loaf of snow,
  We must bide threshing, tribulations sore,
Parting of dross, and heat; the crucial task
 Leaves but a mite of us; yet God, we know,
  Aye lends His strength as tries His fining more.

WHEN COMES THE CROWN?

THE morn breaks gloriously; refreshed with sleep
  The lithe form pauses at the brink of day
  With mind all set for manly toil. We say
He's worthy; but he goes bare-browed to reap.
He's bronzed; the sun has climbed the midday steep;
  The field is treeless; briers line the way
  To cooler places, yet no wreath of bay
Garlands his head. He still must work and weep,
Till evening folds its silken garments round
  His bruised and wearied limbs, and all the spheres
  Break into silent singing. Angels bend
Anear to see him by the Father crowned:
  "Thus shall it be to him who wrought with tears,
  And loved and prayed and trusted to the end."

"AT EVENTIDE IT SHALL BE LIGHT."

THE day is breaking; but the steel
    Of Phœbus' somber livery mars
    The burst of rosy morn; no stars
Pale at the breaking of night's seal.

The air is thick and close; the beech
    And maple droop in listless mood;
    Half-hearted chirps the feathered brood;
Life lags, unthrilled by cordial speech.

The noon sky wears a deeper frown;
    The serried clouds to battle throng
    To war-peal of the thunder's song;
Their strength, full spent, comes raining down.

How heavy lies the afternoon
    Upon the slopes and weeping vales!—
    But mark! the leaden heaven pales;
O, pray the storm be over soon!

The first blue rift of welcome sky
    Grows broader, bluer, till the field
    From bound to bound the war-clouds yield;
In light the evening cometh nigh.

So shall the grief that dims our sight,
    The taunt of pain, the toiling lot,
    In grand deliverance be forgot:
"At eventide it shall be light."

MOTHER AND WIFE.

TWO windows face the highway,
  Two faces guard the panes,
For a loved one's swift home-coming;
  And the rainy daylight wanes.

The hour has struck; he comes not;
  They softly talk awhile,
But silence falls between them;
  Again they watch the stile.

The wife, with poet's fancy
  Sits in a blissful dream
Waiting her lord's returning,
  In her eyes the love-light's beam.

The mother, wrinkled and white-haired,
  Leans on the window-sill,
A smile on her saintly visage,
  Time-worn, yet lovely still.

Which pair of eyes is keener?
  On whom does the vision burst?
One murmurs, "Now he's coming!"
  The mother sees him first!

Ah, yearning heart of a mother!
  Tender as summer skies,
Can wealth of wife's devotion
  Surpass thy sacrifice?

O wife! thy dear gift cherish!
  The mother yields to thee
Her treasure, joy, and comfort;
  Crown thou his destiny.

"AS THE TREE FALLETH."

SO shall it be; whether to North or South
It fall, the chance henceforth shall be its tomb.
  But will it fall by chance? Rare is the stem
Straight-grown to heaven; its pliant grace has leaned
To soft caresses of the sun-land winds,
Or stooped to Arctic rage in shrinking fear.
Which way the restless airs most steady blow
The tree leans too; and this is nature's way.

How will he fall? The world beholds his bent;
Mayhap he's dallied with the gentle breath
Of gilded sin, and thought the touch no harm;
Or some great wish persistent pressed its worth;
Or sips of evil grew to fearless draughts;
And now he hangs over his life's wild brink
Ripe for a plunge into the awful Hence.

How does he lean? Toward the calm, blue sky,
The morning beams of love and generous deeds,
The sunset's eulogy of holiness,
The clouds and rain of faithful chastening,
The rigorous sweep of heaven's bereaving blasts.
So, when the woodman's fateful axe strikes deep,
He falls into the arms of Christ the Lord,
Embosomed in His joy eternally.

WAITING.

SITTING in a well-worn rocker
  Where the twilit silence falls,
Gazing in the crimson firelight
  Tracing phantoms on the walls,
On her face a solemn patience
  Which the shadows partly hide,
Waits a mother for a footstep
  Always due at eventide.

Snows of many weary winters
  Her dark hair have blanched at last;
Troublous winds have blown upon her
  As the years went trooping past;
Waves of care have worn their furrows,
  While the sky of hope hung low,
And her eyes have lost the sparkle
  Once they had so long ago.

As the outer darkness deepens,
  And the hearth-shine brighter grows,
And the busy clock is telling
  That the hour is near its close,
She is looking off to future,
  Sweeping now so sweetly near,
And a strong, light-footed angel
  At the gate she seems to hear.

There is not much more to wait for;
  Just a little suffering yet,
Then the weight that seemed so heavy
  'Twill be easy to forget:
Borne to rest in light-strewn spaces,
  Stars and kingdoms at her feet,
God's best friends will wait upon her,
  And the bliss of heaven repeat.

THE HARP ON THE WILLOW.

O RIVERS of Babylon, grandly ye flow,
　　While sadly we sit by your side;
　　Your clear, welling waters naught whisper of woe,
　　　Yet echo our grief in your tide.
O, Zion, belovèd! for thee do we mourn,
　　While captives afar from thy gates;
Each heart is a tomb for the joys from thee borne,
　　Each harp for its mute player waits.

They tell us to sing,—they, who took us away
　　From thee, blessed city and fair;
But how shall we sing the Lord's anthem, and play,
　　And mirth in our countenance wear?
Our masters are cruel, and strange is the land,
　　For God comes not hither to shine;
Our hearts, nursed in freedom, no joy understand,
　　No glory, O Zion, save thine!

By Babylon's waters the singers sat down;
　　But memory's tide swelled the tear;
Their harps, often sounded their light woes to drown,
　　They hung on the willows anear.
As turns the swift needle to find its own star,
　　To thee, O Jerusalem, bends
The heart of thy people, in bondage afar,
　　And greetings of constancy sends.

THE POPLAR.

STRAIGHT as an arrow sped the shaft
   Into September's sunny blue;
Through its quick leaves the wind-sprites laughed,
   Turning their silver side to view.

As rocking in a listless dream
   I heard the drowsy, waving sound,
Methought that in the careless theme
   A likeness to my life I found.

Now fierce, now soft, now shrill, now low,
   The wandering winds of heaven play
Upon my soul now joy, now woe,
   Now blessed peace, or sorrow gray.

No spirit lives but meets both storm
   And zephyr, pleasure sweet or pain;
Happy the heart whose love-life warm
   Bends to all gales that sweep life's main.

THE ISOTHERMAL LINE.

HOW crooked through the human world it runs!
   On this side all our great and pleasant friends,
   The epauletted swarm of social peers,
The sympathizers with our fond beliefs,
Our wealthy kin, successful geniuses,
A much revised and satisfying list;
On that side, indistinguishable hordes
Of poor and crippled, ignorant and old,
Weak-willed and stupid, selfish and uncouth,
With no horizon but the cheap old walls
Which house their dingy thoughts and dwarf their souls.

This warm love-line, stretched by the hand of God
Straight round the wide equator of His world,
How have we warped upon our petty maps
That do dishonor to His purposes!
The brave Son died for "whosoever's" sake;
His words and help at every hovel called;
"Not many mighty" sought Him as a guest;
But "all the Father's will" He loved and did.
And does his farewell ever trouble us?
"To every creature with my blessing go!"

THE LEPER TOUCHED.

BANNED by the law, in miserable herd,
 He ventured to the public road at sight
 Of numerous passers-by; in beggar's plight,
With gnawn and grewsome limbs, and one dread word,
"Unclean!" he knelt upon the dust, and spurred
 The pity of the Christ; with hand of might,
 Yet soft, and pure, and sweet, He struck the blight;
Lo! fresh and clean the life its course now stirred.
Leprous as he, we haunt the tombs of sin,
 Wasting away, till death were kindest boon;
Cometh this way a Marvelous One, akin
 To God himself; trembling with hope, full soon
We kiss the highway where His dear foot pressed,
Crying, "Make clean!" and—He can tell the rest.

THE SUNSET HARBOR.

THE rain-wet lashes of an April morn
Long since were dry; the Orient sky, aflame
With bravest color, out of midnight born,
Its echo left upon a cheek which came,
Thenceforth, for inspiration to the east,
And loved and worshiped such a marvelous light.

But April died, and June; the sun, released
From morning's clasp, with face more grandly bright
Then strode the heavens, and a girdle bound
Of glory round the busy earth, and man,
With cheek not now ablush, upon the ground
His sterner visage bent and sought a plan
Whereby to garner up the sheaves of light
Into his life, and make it glad and strong.

He planted soon and late, and on a height
Nearest the sun, where lark and linnet's song
Quivered their sweetest, built a fairy nook
And called it home; with wife and merry friend
He thought to live as runs a silver brook
Under the maples till its waters blend
With ocean's everlasting depths.   But hand
And foot grew weary with unfruitful toil
Ofttimes, and drouth and torrid heat the land
Consumed, which mocked the sun, a thankless soil.

Man's heart grew faint; but as his spirit fell
Gazing to eastward for the vanished hues
Of hopeful youth, a wonder broke the spell
Of gloomy faith; the Orient seemed to lose
Its soberness again, and some far gleam
Of gold was mirrored in it; wonderingly
He looked behind him, when behold! a dream
Of poet's paradise upon a sea

Of molten glory swam o'er all the west.
His eyes grew softer with the sun's low dip;
His tired feet, standing on the mountain's crest,
Joy-wingèd grew; he hailed the passing ship
With sun-gilt pennons and with reefs of cloud,
Bound for the port of an eternal calm.

Once more the sun has set; from out the crowd
Of living folk chanting a funeral psalm
A soul has fled beyond the sunset gates
Into the mystic, sweet hereafter; crowned
With rest, the swelling heart no longer waits
To joint the voice and harp in grateful sound.

CIRCLES.

A STAR hurled into space bends on its way
  In strong attraction to the hand that cast
  It forth on errand through the crowded vast,
And brings back word again another day.

A good deed dropped in an untended bed,
  Will take on feet, and wander thro' the earth;
  A thousand seeds of joy will come to birth.
Their fruits return to crown the sower's head.

An evil act springs, goddess-like, full-armed,
  Into the world so human, and returns
  A harvest manifold, that stings and burns
The conscience which the whispering siren charmed.

The thought of man, embodied in his deed,
  Swings to the throne eternal, and recedes,
  Bringing its fruit, or balm, or deadly weeds,
Sharing to each of justice his full meed.

VI.

A ROSARY.

A RUINED ABBEY.

ROOFLESS and silent thro' the dusk it looms;
    Thro' paneless windows the full, mellow moon
    Shines from within; bevies of night-birds croon
Beneath the ivied eaves, whose rich, green glooms,
Constant as seasons, drape forgotten tombs,
    And at the wind's kiss sigh, in solemn rune,
    Of life long gone, and common footprints strewn
Where once the altar burned its rare perfumes.

No angelus breaks from the toppling tower,
    Nor boyish trebles chant the vestal hymn;
The sudden hoot-owl wakes the dead night hour,
    Barbaric minstrel in the gallery dim;
No more the flight of prayer's bright wings we trace;
Time blurs all things; and ruin wraps this place.

MY FORTUNE.

I 'VE read of paintings men called great—
    Inspiring, beautiful, divine;
From dyke-bound Holland, whence the strokes
    Of Rembrandt's heaven-lit genius shine,
To azure, soft-aired Italy,
    Immortalized by Raphael's touch;
And yet their canvases sublime,
    In size nor finish, thrill me much.

I have a gallery of my own,
    With stretches of eternal blue,
Where the Great Painter's wondrous brush
    Makes each perspective fair and new;
The far blue brows bared to the storm,
    The crystal lake kissed by the stars,
The grassy cloth soft to my feet,
    The green world shut with icy bars.

I've read of music festivals,
    Where prima donnas swayed the throng,
Where burst of well-timed orchestras
    Wrought on the soul with pleasure strong;
Where choruses, with solemn swell,
    Their mighty unisons upbore,
But yet their concords move me not
    As those I hear at my own door.

My concerts bide not in one house;
    From zone to zone God's fingers play,
And from the full-responding keys
    Leap out the lark's ethereal lay,
The evening zephyr's dulcet sigh,
    The song of floods, the awful roll
Of thunder's diapason; these
    To the one Artist draw my soul.

JUNE STARS.

WHEN the sun's bright train of hours
    Clambers o'er the western steeps,
And the prayers of the flowers
    Go to God, who never sleeps,
Heaven hangs out her silver moon,
    Lights her astral chandelier,
Sets their twinkle all in tune:—
    Silence!—holy Night is here.

Pure-eyed watchers, far in space,
    Are ye chary of your light?
From the hills we would embrace
    All your rills of glory white;
But ye come not near; aloft
    Ye must shine, while we must tread
Clayey valleys, stumbling oft
    At the Will by which we're led.

Ay, but *must* we? Stars of June,
    Fill us with a silver dream
That shall turn our toil-worn noon,
    From an aching, phantom beam
To a sunny consciousness
    Of the royal worth of days;
Thus your mission's filled no less,
    Thus our hearts enlarge with praise.

ECLIPSED.

THE full, familiar moon now gems the eve
    With mellow glory, borrowed for this night,
When, as the sages say, the world shall weave
    A sudden shroud to veil her virgin light.
The wondrous midnight spectacle we wait,
    Walking at leisure thro' the fresh'ning air;
Save for a strident cricket's vespers late,
    The odorous breeze goes by in silent prayer.

But now dark vapors loom up from the west,
    And anxiously we scan each fading star;
At last our moon is hidden with the rest,—
    Our hopes eclipsed before this misty bar!
But, courage!—yon's a rift; and there's the sky,—
    Clear patches moving swiftly into range;
Here we shall sit until the clouds go by,
    And catch the secret of the mystic change.

Behold! one-half the shining rim is dark;
    A great, round shadow creeps with measure slow,
Like blight untimely choosing fairest mark,
    Across the o'er-bright orb, and blurs its glow.
The latest glimmer's gone; and now a night,
    Blackened and weird, engulfs the sleeping town;
Among the laughing stars of silver light,
    A strange, dead moon is mutely floating down.

Fit hour for contemplation! when the soul
    Awake to heavenly impulse, finds a key
In flashing firmament to read the scroll
    Of God's own graving, signed with His decree.
He kindles suns to light His chambers vast
    And quenches planets at His sovereign will;
He sweeps the mountain tops with Titan blast,
    And whispers to the passionate sea, "Be still!"

Look now! the moon's not banished, after all!
  Her merry face peeps from the other side,
And shakes the shadow from her; soon the pall
  Is lifted from the earth, and faint stars hide
In outstripped glory; nature breathes relief,
  And thankful joy broods o'er the relit scene;
The shine seems brighter for the shadow brief,
  And night's Queen reigns in majesty serene.

CALL TO ACTION.

TOUCH us gently, gray November!
  May these pulsing hearts remember
  Nothing from thy visitation
  Save a rich and rare collation,—
  Feast of privilege and pleasure,
  Founts of truth too deep to measure.

  Life is never stale to workers,
  But is freshened every moment
  By the conscious acquisition
  Of reward for toil invested.
  Only drones for peace are sighing;
  Rest to them's a sound unmeaning;
  Like the gossamer in autumn,
  Clinging to the weeds and corn-stalks,
  They are floating 'mid the harvests,
  Hanging to the skirts of labor.

  Youth, be wise! your fate keeps calling;
  Work and faith will save your falling.

AD BELLUM.

A GOLDEN, glad June morning
   Broke o'er the city vast;
An early train was speeding
   Suburban villas past;
Once, while it halted briefly,
   There blithely stepped on board
A file of youthful soldiers
   With knapsacks newly stored.

Their uniforms were faultless,
   Their guns and bayonets bright,
Their drums and horns, though silent,
   Held spurs for valorous fight ;
Their faces, glad and healthful,
   Told how the warm heart beat,
Nor guessed, I trow, what perils
   Wait for all war-shod feet.

One lad, with mien so gentle,
   With eye of heavenly blue,
With modest smile and winsome,
   My chief attention drew;
"Brow for a mother's kisses!"
   I thought; and wondered when
The mother-heart would welcome
   The darling son again.

O ruthless war! that plucks the rarest prize,
That cleaves a home, and dims a woman's eyes;
Hence with thy horrid hoofs! and leave us hold
Our brothers, husbands, sons, better than gold.

TWO SKIES.

I STOOD upon the river shore
  Enraptured with the crystal tide;
Its bed a tint of turquois wore,
  With cloud-veil, fit for river's bride!

The mirror, with its changeful grace,
  Was upward turned; my eyes turned too
The fair original to trace;
  O, fleecy trails o'er heavenly blue!

O, happy river! whose clear breast
  Reflects the canvas of the sky,
Be thou my teacher; it is best
  To image joy as life flits by.

TWILIGHT SONG.

TWILIGHT falls through the halls
  As the sun hides in the west;
Far on wing, birds that sing
  Now in dreamy tree-tops rest.

Sweet the air everywhere;
  Blossoms breathe their evening prayer;
Stars so white pin the night
  O'er the sleepy earth so fair.

Drowsy heads downy beds
  With their slumbrous balm invite;
Good-night, friends; sleep God sends;
  Rest and sleep, dear world; good-night.

MY SERVANTS.

BLANK darkness paints the woodland sky;
I cannot see the way;
Lo! from the rosy-lidded east
Winks the round eye of day!

I'm weary of this pebbly stretch,
The hard-blue heat and calm;
Ha! comes the fresh'ning west wind up
And laves my face with balm.

The grass and I, in dusty coat,
Look upward, limp with thirst;
At once a clear rill dimples by,
And showers from full skies burst!

Here's a hard seed; I want a flower;
I hide it in the mold,
Till sun and dews—strange alchemy!—
A wondrous bloom unfold.

I want to visit with my friend
Across the continent;
My steed of steam halts at his door,
With fire and strength unspent.

I reach one day a precious goal;
I'll let the home-folks know;
The lightning cries, "Hurrah, send me!"
So back the glad words go.

I want a draught of pure, deep joy;
I call the central 'Phone;
God's voice rings sweetly back, "I come!
I bring it from my throne!"

IN THE WHEAT-FIELD.

INTO the fields my Master went
　At judgment-harvest; here, and here,
The yellow stems with heads down-bent,
　He girdled tenderly; his dear,
Bright face looked all about, and o'er
　The swath his gleaners still found gold,
And sheaf by sheaf brought in the store
　And into shocks of sunshine rolled.

I grew there too; my stem was straight,
　But not grain-laden like the rest;
The Master saw my empty state
　And tossed me from him; in their quest
The gleaners did not find me.　Grief
　Now darkens all the field, nor sing
The larks henceforth; signs force belief:
　I was not worth the gathering!

　　　*　　*　　*　　*　　*

O Master, is it true?
O tell me, is it true?

MUSIC.

THE uncreate Voice, whose thrill dead chaos clove;
　The answers of all winds, and birds, and deeps;
The meeting in mid-sky of faith and Love;
　An angel's footfall when a baby sleeps.

THE MYSTERIOUS RECITAL.

(Paraphrase of a prose sketch.)

MONKISH shadows from the forest,
  When the summer sun went down,
Draped the time-used monastery,
  Blotted out the mountain's frown;
Sailing on the blue, blue Danube,
  Past dark woods and convents high,
Two had been since early morning,
  Till faint vespers chimed near by.

Quickly landed, child and father
  Sought the hooded monks to know
If the night they might abide there
  Just above the river's flow;
Cheery words assured them welcome,
  Gave them hearty, homespun fare,
Lodged them in a spacious chamber,
  Carved, and hung with paintings rare.

Ere the cloister shades grew dimmer
  Spoke the father to the son,
"Woferl, wouldst thou see the organ?"
  Gleefully assent was won;
Thro' the chapel's aisle they wandered,
  Reached and climbed the organ stairs,
Stood before the pipes and pedals,—
  Voice for human thanks and prayers.

Filled with wide-eyed joy and wonder,
  Little "Woferl" raised his head
To his elder for a moment:—
  "Father, let me play," he said.
With his prompt and pleased permission
  He approached the silent keys,

Stepped upon the mighty pedals,
  Rapt, as one who visions sees.

Then his tiny, charmèd fingers
  Swept the key-board full and fast,
Woke the soul within the organ
  Thrilled with concord new and vast.
Peal on peal of chords triumphant
  E'en the chapel shadows stirred;—
March, and dirge, and joyous anthem,
  Chirp, and trill, and flight of bird.

But the spirit of the music
  By the wondrous child set free,
Thro' the monastery trembled
  Like a billowed, sounding sea,—
Reached the quiet monks at supper,
  Who, at sounds so sweet and strong,
Dropped their hands and gazed astonished;
  Could such strains to earth belong?

Rising from their meal unfinished,
  Thro' the dusky halls they stole,
But within the chapel halted,
  Hearing still the organ's roll.
"'Tis the evil one," they whispered,
  And they shrank from going near
To the mystic organ-player;
  Stood, and held their breath for fear.

Then the bravest one took courage,
  Seized a light, and called the rest;
So they climbed the steep old stairway,
  And the mystery was guessed!
Child-musician, Wolfgang Mozart!
  Browed with genius' heaven-born gleam,
May thy angelhood of music
  Fill thy childhood's sweetest dream.

BY WAY OF THE EARTH.

ONE day there was a sad good-by in heaven;
　　The King's delight, his only child, took off
　　His princely purple and the diadem
That crowned his lustrous hair; with tender clasp
He took each angel's hand who sorrowing came
To gaze once yet into their favorite's face;
And last his dear, good Father comforted
With filial kiss and lingering, strong embrace.
Nor scrip nor barest purse took he in hand;
Of all divested save his own sweet soul,
He started down the golden pavement; then,
All heaven's adoring eyes toward him astrain,
They saw him passing out the gate alone.

One night, among the crowd at Bethlehem,
A stranger sought the inn; a fledgeling fair,
O'er whom his mother wondered, crooned, and smiled.
On the cool hills, where drowsy sheep lay safe
Beside their wakeful keepers, such a scene
Burst 'mid the quiet stars as brought to mind
Their choral at the daybreak of the world.
The corners of the vibrant sky were full
Of new-come angel forms, whose spokesman thus
The arrival of the heavenly Prince announced;
"In yonder town the Hope of all men lies;
A babe new-born, your Saviour, Christ the Lord."

Scarce had the music of his welcome died
When he was carried, by a midnight road,
To Egypt, safe asylum from the burst
Of jealousy that wrapped in sables dire
All Bethlehem's cradles. In that southern air
He nestled, till the messenger angel came
And gave his foster-father this brief word:—

124

"Go, take the infant and his mother home;
  For they are dead who thirsted for his life."

The marvel of his advent faded soon
From people's memories; but now the Child
Began to brush the must and cobwebs down
Of temple doctrine, and redeem the way
Wherein might walk the lonely Son of God.
Around the homestead ranged his restless feet,
While on his mother's Scripture roll he mused,
Till on a day, with all his powers full-blown,
With every detail of his journey planned,
He walked out 'neath the sky, a homeless Man.

In desert bantered by the breath of sin;
In quiet mountains praying all the night;
Fatigued with blessing begging multitudes;
On Galilee's rough bosom fast asleep;
Resting upon the well-curb in the heat
Of Sychar's noon, with gracious offering
Of satisfying draft from heaven's own spring;
Granting a glimpse of glory scarcely hid
By his earth body, to a close-knit three;
On little children's heads, with tender palms,
A benison pronouncing; from the mob
Catching rebuke, or curse, or wild hurrah;
Finding repose of body and of soul
In Bethany's devout, delightful home;
In royal progress entering his own
Loved capital; in errands to and fro
Comfort and mercy measuring to all;
Hasting to finish his high embassage
Before returning to his Father's house;
Without the gate, deep in the olive grove
Where ominous midnight hung, with all the weight

Of all the world's sin prostrate; angel-helped,
Rising again to take his last few steps;
Standing thorn-bound, amid the shameless stabs
Of ridicule; his soft, white shoulder bruised
With great, rough-timbered cross unflinching borne
To Golgotha; with dumb lips suffering
Thro' six hours' awful rack; with day's light quenched,
Nature aghast at such a spectacle,
His tired soul passing thro' earth's exit gate,
Glad to begin his upward journey home.

"Watchman, what news?" With strong eyes earthward
        bent,
The lookout on the jasper wall espied
A soft cloud rising, on its bosom white
A road-stained traveler riding; the old smile,
Sweetly familiar to all angelkind,
Beamed up at him; the recognition burst
Like some lost fragrance on his delicate sense;
Swift rang his trumpet down the splendid street,
"Swing wide the door, and bring an escort strong!
The darling of our life is come again!"

Ah, then the listless harps were quickly strung,
And silvery voices sparkled with new notes,
And all the city massed toward the gate.
And when at last the nail-scarred feet had pressed
The golden sill, such welcome over rang,
As shook the leaves that shaded all the way
Up to the throne; with soft solicitude
They marked the quiver of the shapely hand,
The red brand of the earthy bigot brood,
As each one begged to hold it; tender arms
Him fairly lifted from the burnished floor,
While in his ears the gentle chorus rang:
"It was so lonesome while you were away!"

As on they trooped, with glad processional,
They met the Father, who his sovereign seat
One supreme moment vacant left to fall
In transport on his Well-beloved's neck;
"O Son, mine only one, my life returned!"

TO THE FULL MOON.

HAIL, calm-faced orb! with diadem of stars,
    Majestic rising in thy wonted place,
    Whose eyes the tombs of sleeping ages trace,
What scenes have met thy patient-shining bars!
Anon 'twas carnage on the field of Mars;
    Then meads and mountains, clad in silent grace;
    Or lakes, where lovers watched thy mirrored face;
Or dark blue tides and decks with sun-browned tars.

This rough old world learns peace from thy mild
            brow;
    Men's hate dies out beneath thy mellow beam;
No goddess wears more generons smile than thou,—
    To gird the dark from birth has been thy dream.
The heritage of youth is quickly gone;—
Serene and silvern still thy light burns on.

THE ADVENTURER.

WITHOUT the well-worn threshold of the sky
  Saint Peter, turnkey for dim centuries,
    A clamorous knocking heard; the golden gate
On noiseless hinge he turned, and fronting him,
With hair disheveled, scarred and bruisèd limbs
From hasting up the fiercely-chasmed cliff,
A recent mortal quivering stood; with swift
And trenchant gaze the turnkey measured him.
"What dost thou here before thy time?" he asked.
"O good Saint Peter, I was tired of life;
  The world discovered me in hidden deed;
  My soul sank 'neath the whisperings of scorn,
Heartless; I took the near cut from it all,
And thro' the rear door fled the open stage
And ran up hither; take me in, I pray."

The warder of the fateful portal kept
His hand upon the latch, and said: "In all
God's golden empire there is not a nook
For any save whom He has called what time
It pleased Him, with His own escort; like thee,
Hundreds have begged me for a place within,
Bearing the brand of violated law,
'Thou shalt not kill.' I have my orders clear;
The world and time were given thee to prepare;
There is no place for penance here." So said,
Saint Peter shut the great gate in his face.

THE STORY OF CHARLOTTE CORDAY.

(Paraphrase of a prose sketch.)

RICH glowed the sunset o'er Normandy's corn-fields,
  Painting one evening a century gone,
Lighting a convent at Caen, by the river
  Orne, that, gold-glinted, to seaward ran on.

Stood by a casement a beautiful maiden,—
  Hair kissed with sunshine and eyes darkly blue,
Form tall and womanly, face classic-featured,
  Soul sweet as angel's, devotion as true !

Softly her lips with warm orisons parted ;
  Shoreless and deep was her love, like the sea;
Child of the summer, in joy and peace nurtured,—
  Dreamed one the deed France should tremble to see ?

*   *   *   *   *   *   *

Year followed year, till a decade brought changes.
  Drenched was the land in a baptism of blood;
Throned on a scaffold sat sovereign Terror,
  Dooming fresh victims to swell the red flood.

Changed, too, the heart of the beautiful maiden;
  Love for one being had filled all her soul;
Now all her soul with one hate was impassioned:
  "France, retribution, then death,—welcome goal!

"Red shall the sacrifice be for my lover,
  Friends dear and kindred the tyrant has slain;
Mine be the hand that, unknown, shall undaunted
  Blot from the country this inhuman stain!"

Forth on the morrow to Paris she traveled,
  Guarded alone by her righteous design.
Marveled the passengers much at her beauty;—
  One heart impulsively knelt at its shrine.

Curious, they questioned her whither she journeyed;
  Asked of her friends in the city, and where
Lived they ; but wisely the maiden made answer,
  Smiles on her lips, but her heart full of prayer.

Night brought the dawn; and the fair girl's compan-
      ions,
  Bent to determine her mission, alone,
Toward the heart of the dread revolution,
  Talked of Marat,—how his power had grown.

Watched they for sign in the maiden's sweet features,
  While they extolled that most monstrous of men,
Whether her sympathies lived with the people
  Or with the kingdom; a lovely smile then

Played on her lips, with her cheeks faintly flushing;
  "Links not your cause with the people's?" one cried;
"Yes," was her answer, "the people forever!"
  Thus much she spoke; her face only replied

When the enthusiasts cried in a chorus,
  "Long live the 'Friend of the People,' Marat!"
Smiled she again, but her soul felt a shudder;
  Stanch grew her purpose for vengeance and law.

Three days had passed; and the diligence rattled
  Into the city; how little they thought
Who with this beautiful lady had chatted,
  History's page with her fame should be fraught!

Whispered the one whom her graces had conquered,
  As to the roar of the city they came,
That, tho' unknown, she had wakened such passion,
  Prompting his offer of heart and of name.

"Nay, friend," she laughed, "I deserve not such
   bounty;
   Wait till you know me, then study your heart;"
Then, as he prayed she would some time reward him,
   Bowed him farewell; so they drifted apart.

Threading the streets of the blood-flowing city
   After a rest from the journey's long strain,
Entered she boldly the shops of the cutlers,
   Seeking a tool to rid France of its bane.

Found she at last a keen, glittering poniard,
   Deftly the steel in her bosom concealed;—
Beautiful Nemesis! armed for love's vengeance,
   Love's and her country's;—ay, Terror must yield!

   *   *   *   *   *   *   *

Entered the beams of the morrow's rich sunset
   Into a chamber dark, dingy, and old,
Fell on a form fitter mated with demons,
   Lit up his face with brute frenzy controlled.

Rapidly wrote the grim, bloodthirsty monster
   Names of the doomed, with their blood to be
      sealed;—
Suddenly voices an entrance disputed;—
   What silver tones to his stained soul appealed?

"Ay, I must see this great Friend of the People!
   Twice have I written him, begging to tell
News for the safety of France, now imperiled!"
   "Ay, let her pass, my dear; serves her zeal well."

Thus to his housekeeper called the gaunt tyrant.
   Stood then before him a vision so rare,
Radiant and queenlike, in white, fleecy drapings,
   Crowned by the sunset her own golden hair,

That at the sight for a moment he wondered;
  Then, gloating on her, he said, "Tell me all;
Caen is your home, says your letter; what traitors
  Lurking in Normandy can you recall?"

"Many, great citizen," softly she answered;
  Then at his signal gave name after name,
Which with an ecstasy fiendish he listed,
  Keener for blood than the wolf for its game.

"These are all," finally murmured the stranger.
  "Well, 'tis a goodly roll, thanks to your aid;
Ere a week passes, their heads shall roll lightly
  Under the stroke of the guillotine's blade!"

"Guillotine!" quietly echoed the maiden,
  Raising her hand to her bosom, the while
Fixing her eye on the heart of the monster
  Striking the list with a hideous smile.

Moment supreme! with the spring of a tigress
  Raised she the steel in the flash of the sun,
Buried it deep in the criminal's life-blood,
  And flung it down, dripping;—its mission was done.

"Help!" he groaned once; and the angel of vengeance
  Saw at her feet the dead scourge of the land.
But in an instant a terrible uproar
  Swept to the door at that startling command.

Dashed to the floor was the beautiful maiden,
  Trampled and cursed by the rabble, whose cries
Echoed to drum-beat and firing of cannon;
  Thrilled was the city with angry surprise.

*   *   *   *   *   *   *

Willing to die a swift victim to fury,
    Yet for four days was her trial delayed;
Finished her work for her country's salvation;
    What matter now how long death for her stayed?

Once more the sun of midsummer was setting;
    Proudly the doomed maiden went forth alone;
Rudely the headsman the fair head uplifted;
    Redly the sun on the sacrifice shone.

A SUNSET THOUGHT.

THE woods are afire at the top of the hill!
I sit here and watch the red burning so still;
Scarce heard are the sounds of the fresh-throbbing
        spring,
Or song which the home-coming laborers bring.
Down, down to the roots creeps the rich, crimson
        blaze,
And pink bars run up on the gray evening haze.
A last tiny sparkle—the day's eye is closed;
Good-night, dear old sun! unto sweet rest disposed;
Good-bye! till the starlight is over;—but then—
Suppose I shall never your face see again?
Ah, then, may a blesseder morning be mine,
When over my waking heaven's glory shall shine;
And up like a bird whom the spring dawnings call,
I'll run to my Master, the Light of it all!

133

VII.

THE RED CALENDAR.

IS THE NEW YEAR HAPPY?

LAST night the old year died. The rest were all
    asleep,
  Yet slumber wooed me not; I saw the white moon
    peep
With solemn face within my chamber, and the wail
And sob of winds rehearsed the old impressive tale.

A rasping, choking moan about the gables swept,
And gloom and tears around the old year's bedside
    crept;
A dying look stole o'er the ripe old veteran's face,
He shivered once, and then—his spirit left the place.

Ah, me! old year, thy life was charged with many a joy
And sorrow, too; for mortal gladness with alloy
Is ever mixed; yet has thy sojourn not been vain
If we have learned a lesson in the school of pain.

"A Happy New Year!" With the morning's crispy
    dawn
The rooms were swept and ordered, and the grave-clothes
    gone;—
Around a little crib we pressed a happy while,
To catch the primal light of baby New Year's smile.

And is it happy? Does it bring us all delight?
Surely, the morning's fresh, the broad old sun is bright;
The only cloud I saw was at the break of day,
But ere the streets woke up, I saw it melt away.

Yet was it not suggestive? Other New Year's days
Have beamed as rosy, and diffused as happy rays,
But shadows followed after; love, grief, hope and fear,
Close-ranked, filed by, in the procession of the year.

But can we not be happy always? 'Tis to me
A sweet and constant song, untuned to minor key,
To do my loving, faithful utmost; for my guide,
A gracious sky gives pledge that God is satisfied.

THE MYSTERY IN THE GARDEN.

AN EASTER WONDER.

HERE is the open crypt, where late
Soft hands immured a dear, dead form;
Sweetly He slept, in humble state,
After the burst of envy's storm;
Wound in the grave's white vestments, laid
In pleasant odors, stone and seal
He marked nor recked; in that awed shade
The very silence fain would kneel.

But things are rent; the breaking day
   Looks in upon an empty bed;
Where last night lay the precious clay,
   The folded habit lies instead;
How came the strong door open so?
   Who took these clothes from off the dead?
And where is He? These low walls know,
   That echoed His departing tread.

How did He rise? Did angels bend
   To lift Him and return his soul
Now three days gone? Did they descend
   The close-wrapped cerements to unroll,
And lead Him forth a free, new man?
   What shook the earth? With what defense
Met He the guard? What wondrous plan
   Lies in the mystic exit hence?

Flashes the *Word* across the dark;
   "I am the Resurrection; though
Entombed a marble Christ, the spark
   Of life immortal now doth glow
By mine own will; whoso believes
   The mystery, the same shall rise
When I shall come to bind my sheaves,
   And solve the secret in the skies."

AN EASTER GLEAM.

OUT of the awe-struck night,
Loosing the tomb's dark might,
Flasheth a wondrous light,
    Born ere the day;
Lighting the garden wall,
Waking the night-bird's call,
Softly the glad beams fall,
    Then speed away.

Look! has the Son awoke?
See! are the sure seals broke?
Yes! like a heaven-rent oak
    Standeth the tomb;
Forth in the garb of white,
Looped with the tints of light,
Cometh the Man to sight,
    Thrilled with life's bloom.

Over the paling sky
Spreadeth the brightness high;
Quickly the hills reply
    With echoing sheen;
Catch the far mounts the glow,
Shimmer the peaks of snow,
Quiver all zones that know
    Aught of this scene.

Day of the ages, hail!
Rent is the mystic veil;
Vigils nor rocks avail
    To keep our dead;
Starred with all grace Thy brow,
Hope of the world art Thou;
Greet we the Conqueror now,—
    Our Strength, our Head.

AN EASTER SEPULCHER.

THE broad, still-flowing river
    Is wrapped in a winding-sheet;
The rising sunbeams pierce it,—
    It lifts, and morning's feet
Come treading down the hill-slopes,
    And up the quiet street,
And into curtained chambers,
    The Easter world to greet.

How swollen are the leaf-buds !
    Rare peach and cherry bloom
Shed on the early landscape
    Their color and perfume;
The dewy grass, green-tufted,
    Throws back the sun's bright face;
The warm south-wind is waking
    From the solemn night's embrace.

A hushed assembly's gathered
    Round a baptismal tomb;
A soul is brought to burial,
    Shrouded in sin's dark doom;
With Christ the water's entered;
    To Christ the dead soul clings,
And lo! to resurrection
    Reanimated springs!

Best morning of the ages!
    The birthday of our hope,
When tombs and hearts and blossoms
    God's finger-touches ope;
The Son of glory beameth
    Upon the sea of woe;
To sorrow's depths love streameth,
    And faith leaps from below.

O, dawn of joy inwoven!
　　With mind and sense and soul
We clasp thy message to us,
　　And drink thy brimming bowl;
God of all times and seasons
　　And human destiny,
Call us from sleep to singing,
　　And let us rise to Thee!

REQUIEM.

SOFTLY tread; this ground is holy;
　　Here our sainted neighbors sleep;
O'er their couch, so still and lowly,
　　God's own stars their vigils keep.

When the reaper angel found them,
　　Some were sheaves for garner meet;
Some were tender buds of promise,
　　But he bound them with the wheat.

On this day of birds and blossoms,
　　Lay your garlands on their breast;
May their memory be fragrant
　　Till we all have gone to rest!

IN PRAISE OF TREES.

AMONG the noble things of earth
   High ranks the stately tree;
In vernal grace it tops the hills,
   Where deer run wild and free;
The meadow landscape soothes the eye,
   With silver willows dressed;
While beechen groves, like body-guards,
   Stand round the dear home nest.

The branches catch the passing winds
   And let their music float,
While in the swaying, dizzy tops
   Is heard the wild-bird's note;
In storm they break the north-wind's bow,
   In heat their shelter lend;
In wood or field, or roadside gray,
   Their use and beauty blend.

Let every heart whom Nature charms
   And comforts on this day,
And he who would a kindness do,
   An honest tribute pay;
Seek out some spot of verdure bare,
   Break up the stony ground;
There plant a tree, and soon with joy
   Your labor will be crowned.

PATRIOT'S SONG.

O LAND of our birth, blessed home of the free!
Our voices we mingle to celebrate thee.
We rest 'neath the wings of the eagle outspread,
And cheer the old banner that floats overhead.

O pride of our fathers, Columbia the grand!
With pledge of devotion united we stand;
No nation so happy, so thriving, so blest;
Hurrah for our country, the pride of the West!

O cradle of liberty, rocked in the storm,
For thee may thy children's affection be warm;
To thee may we rally should danger impend,
In voice and in action thine honor defend.

O flag of our union! O, red, white, and blue!
To thy precious colors we'll always be true;
Shine on, silver stars! o'er the farthermost sea,
And tell all the world of Columbia, the free.

GIVING AND TAKING.

A THANKSGIVING INCIDENT.

T HE skies were wet and murky,
The streets were patched with snow,
The beaded pines like friars
In silence stood a-row;
With reverent gladness thronging
Up to the holy place
Came blooming men and women
To praise God's liberal grace.

144

What recked the rosy children
　　That sunless broke the day?
In furry gowns and mufflers
　　They churchward led the way;
Their boundless faith brought visions
　　Of boards with plenty piled,
Where aunts and uncles chatted
　　And pretty cousins smiled.

But as in thankful quiet
　　I walked the gray street thro',
A somber, brief procession
　　Came slowly into view;
Black veils and tear-wet kerchiefs
　　Their simple tale betrayed;
Within a tiny casket
　　Their joy the weepers laid.

As gravely thro' the village
　　The modest cortege paced,
I turned to look, and wondered
　　What thanks the sad wheels traced;
Did God call that a blessing
　　To take the babe away,
And did the mourners praise Him
　　For such a dreary day?

Our poor blind eyes are worthless
　　To show us God's best deeds;
Our earth-bound hearts are useless
　　To learn our sternest needs;
So whether glad or heart-wrung,
　　Our song should be the same:
"The Lord hath given and taken,
　　And blessed be His name!"

THE angels are at rare employ today;
  The bowers are mute whose rosy roofs are stirred
  Most times with harmony of harps; the word
Runs thro' the realm: "To th' earthward gate, straight-
    way!"
The happy hosts their comrades' call obey;
 "A present for His Majesty!" is heard;
  By willing hands the freight is soon transferred
To golden vials, ranged on jeweled tray.
Up the broad, shining pavement, toward the throne,
  The lading shouldered, the fleet cherubs come;
    Around the King ambrosial odors rise
Of prayers distilled in earth's Thanksgiving zone;
  He speaks!--"Of all love-songs this is the sum;
    Strike your antiphonies thro' Paradise!"

GIFTS.

OUT of the solemn night-time, voiced by the choral
    stars,
  Stealeth a sky-born cadence down from its lattice
      bars:
"*Gloria in excelsis!* peace and good will on earth;
Out of His great heart's pity cometh a Christ to birth!"

Gift of all time and nations! sacrifice wide and free!
Sum of all thought unselfish, more than all loves that be;
Infinite wealth of comfort, treasure of joy and rest,
Fair as the heart of heaven, warm as the Father's breast.

Labors of all creation loyally serve God's will;
"This is my law forever; *giving* shall all fulfil."
So, from the gray-spun rain-cloud streameth its own
      life down,
Filling the golden wheat-ears, washing the dusty town.

Rivers the rain-pearls gather, sending their freight to
      sea;
Back to the sky's pale fleeces climbs the blue spray in
      glee;
Trees for their gracious baptism blossom and fruit be-
      stow;
Flowers for crystal kisses buried in perfume blow.

Over the soft blue concave poureth a great gold light,
Life of the world-old day-god, riding with strength be-
      dight;
So giveth every star-point gladly its meed of grace;
Sweetly the pale moon follows, benisons in her face.

Out of a human loving springeth full many a gift,
Seeking, perhaps, to gather some hopeless soul adrift;
And there's a heartless bounty, currently told of men,
That, though their purse gives grandly, much they expect
      again.

Oh, for the sense of nature! always to give our best,
Solely for God's dear glory, leaving to Him the rest;
Sacrifice fills the measure; happiness waits the deed;
Thus shall the Christ-Child's kingdom over the earth
      make speed.

CHRISTMAS WAITS.

SILVERY chime-bells from turret and tower
   Fling their blithe peals on the still morning air;
   Ring the deep tones o'er the dark belfry stair
Out on the town; 'tis a glad, holy hour.

Peal the huge pipes in the cloister's gray light,
   Trembling with melody slow and sublime;
   Mounting the arches with soul-thrilling rhyme,
Melt the sweet chords in their shadowy height.

Far up the azure, in majesty hang
   All the bright orbs that forever rehearse
   God and his love; and we echo the verse—
"Peace and good wishes!"—the morning stars sang.

Why floats such music across the dim earth?
   What early watchers surround the church-door?
   These, ah! they harbor some wonderland lore,
And chant in their service a Prince-royal's birth.

Lived He in honor, in purple and gold,
   Sceptered and crowned with His subjects' regard?
   Made He wise laws, which some young, loyal bard
Storied in verse, thro' the centuries old?

Nay; not a rich, jeweled monarch was He;
   Shrined in poor hearts was his noblest estate;
   Gave He his life-blood to fierce human hate,
Died while He murmured, "Forgive them for me."

Hark! hear the waits sing the chorus again;
   Join hosts of angels the swelling refrain,
   Linking to heaven the sweet, fading strain:
"Glory to God in the highest, Amen!"

LINES FOR A CHRISTMAS SOUVENIR.

AS down a sunbeam slips the wondrous song
    Which angels love to chant at this dear time,
I catch their mood and in my heart prolong
    The thought of Love, a soft, sweet Christmas chime;
Love means a gift; divinest of the throng
    Is he who imitates the Love sublime.

A CHRISTMAS VERSE.

EVER the skies grow deeper,
    And brighter the star-shine glows,
As breaketh this birth-night o'er us
    To welcome fair Sharon's Rose.

149

VIII.

ON OCCASIONS.

A PHILOPENA.

(To F. L. W.)

NOT German maid, in gracious league to pay
    The forfeit of her slip to him who shares
    The sweet, twin-kerneled almond, bravelier wears
The air of debtor on that ill-starred day
Than I on this; take, friend, my gift, I pray,
  In which I fold a wish that no wild tares
  May doubtful harvest bring thee, whose life bears
Such pledge of generous gleaning by the way.
'Twas but a passing thought proposed the sign;
  The morsel eaten—'twas a trifle too;
But as gross things more subtle may define,
  So this suggests an inner, homelike view
Of prim acquaintance; 'tis not hard to make
Chance wayside friends by rule of "give and take."

TO MY MOTHER.

(On her seventy-third birthday.)

OUT of winter clouds and bareness
May this day bring joy and comfort
To thy gentle heart, dear mother,—
Wrap thee round with mellow sunshine!

On thy long and tedious journey
Rest a moment at this mile-stone,
Looking toward the gates of sunset.
From thy youth now dim in distance
To this moment thou hast traveled,
Oft thro' stony ways and shadows,
Yet with sun-gleams thro' the cloud-rifts.
As thou sittest by the hearth-fire
May thy retrospect remind thee
Not of aches and cares perplexing,
But of Him whose tender mercy
Helped thee bear them all in patience;
Brought thee safely to this birthday.

Though the wide world never knew thee,
Yet my loyal heart is witness
To thy constant sacrificing,
To thy uncomplaining spirit,
And the meek content that rules thee,
Thee, the kindest, best of mothers!

God our blessed Father keep thee
Each short mile yet stretching onward,—
Only He can know how many
Till thy feet shall pass the turn-stile
On the verge of the eternal.

Look where now the sunset chariots
Decked with gold and crimson banners
Wheel around thy western hill-top.

Each new day they're nearer, brighter;
And when thy last step is measured,
And thy faithful work is ended
In the world so full of trouble,
Thou wilt find an angel waiting
With a message from the Master:
"Come up now; thy heaven is ready."

In His fragrant, fruitful gardens
He will lead thee by still waters,
Give thee rest in cool, green pastures,
And provide thee peace and gladness
By His loving hand forever!

OCTOBER 18.

(To B. C. U.)

IN the autumn's gold tiara,
Set with regal show of brilliants,
On her flushed and ample forehead
This thy natal day doth sparkle
Red, like days once crimson-lettered
Marking men and deeds distinguished.
Like the fullness of the harvests,—
Faithful vineyards, purple-laden,
Wide-spread trees, with good cheer bending,
Billowy wheat-fields, glad and golden,—
May the ripening of thy service
For the beautiful and noble,
For the kindling of devotion,
Be a crown upon thy temples,
A content about thy fireside,
And an anthem to thy spirit.
May our Father find thy dwelling,
And His blessing light upon thee!

TO MY HUSBAND.

(On being separated from him on his birthday.)

AS the April sun comes laughing
With a teardrop on its lashes
On this morn of old acquaintance,
May it find thee full of courage
And in cheerfulness reposing,
While God's angels sit beside thee
Keeping thee in health and comfort.

Many leagues to-day we're sundered;
But our tender, lingering heart-clasp
Knoweth naught of time or distance,
Bridging all the roughened valley
'Tween the hill-tops of our look-out.
At thy post I still desire thee,
Treading duty's daily turnings,
Always generous meed bestowing,
As our Master sets example.
Yet—how wistfully I'm scanning
O'er the calendar for summer,
Seeking for a rose-lined morning
When my faith to sight shall quicken,
And once more you'll stand before me
As you stood my plighted sweetheart!

Rest in peace, my dearest husband;
May our Father's smile caress thee,
Keep thee pure, direct and shield thee,
And may all who learn to know thee
Be thy helpers and thy pleasure!

GOD HOLDS US ALL.

(To W. J. S.)

"TAKE me, papa," said my darling,
　　As we stood within the hall;
So I bore him up the stairway,
　　Scarcely felt the burden small.

In my other hand I carried
　　Books I wished to scan that night,
And the elfin begged me let him
　　Take them in his arms so slight.

Step by step to top we mounted;
　　Then he said with childish pride,
"Baby carried books for papa,—
　　Didn't he?" "Yes," I replied.

Little innocent! ne'er dreaming,
　　As he bore the asked-for load,
That his father's strength upheld him,
　　Double-burdened on the road.

God is sometimes pleased to give us
　　Work for wondrous skill and thought;
Gleefully we don the laurels,
　　When *His* hand the triumph wrought.

"SURGE, LUCE!"

(To K. P., a school comrade, promoted May 22, 1884.)

BUT yestere'en we sat and talked awhile.
Talked, as our wont, in sweet and hopeful strain,
Of days agone, that bore, with fingers mild,
The benisons of friendship, peace and faith;
Of Time's dim promise for the future, when
In fuller gladness and enlargèd power
We both might work and honor womankind,
Exalt the truth, and Heaven's approval win.
It was but now I heard her blithe voice speak;
From her dear eyes looked out a light that came
Down from the deep and bright immensity
Where stars sailed slow and queen-like, and the flood
Of rose-hued sunset mellowed all the West.
The calm night thrilled us; and forthwith arose
Upon our lips a psalm of David's harp.
She sang a tender treble; and I hush
My heart-throbs now, to catch its closing strain.

O, oft and cheery were her sweet, clear notes,
As trilling now the warblings of the wood,
While sunbeams played upon her face, and now
Responsive chords awaking by the slow
And deeper tones of worship, she infused
The warmth of social feeling and forgot
Her own sad crosses, borne in secret hours.
Full well we all her sunny patience praised;
And humble confidence she sacred kept.
Right gladsome sped the time in lively chat
With her, the queen and flower of our loves.

Ah, heavy fell the news of mystic change—
That Death's pale messenger had borne her hence!

The words felt cold as lead, and sudden tears
Sprang from their fount, and shut all else away.
O, "Pure one," hast thou gone and left me here?
O, art thou dead? They tell me so, and yet
Thy recent smile and going in and out
Makes stern, hard truth seem false, and thou dost live.
But, nay; I'm forced to that dread fact, and see
The funeral train slow pacing to thy tomb.

Each heart wore sables; 'mid the general woe
And tears and wailing, e'en the heavens were sad
And gentle drops of sympathy fell down
Upon earth's bosom, near whose mother-heart
They laid her sacred casket. O, the long,
The last, fond gaze, when grief, unmixed with self,
Hung o'er that face, in victor's triumph wreathed.
White-petaled flowers, fit emblem of her life,
Their fragrant incense brought; and on her breast
Sweet lilies-of-the-valley loving lay.
And now her form is lowered; now, in firm
Yet easy throws, six school-mates' manly hands
The clods replace, and sadly fill the grave.
The green mounds near bespeak a tender thought;
Our love's repose their company shall keep.
There; leave we now this hallowed burial-place;
She sleeps unharmed in Salem's quiet shade.

Is this the end? O stars, and moon, and sun,
We look up to you now in dearer awe,
Because of God's sweet promise that the pure
Shall shine, full-orbed, in royal magnitude.
No, Death's a messenger; our love's not dead,
But left her little world of friends and kin,
Pupils and classmates, all the dearest links
That drew her loving soul to earth, and leaped
On joy's swift pinions, far up through the blue,

Bright floor of heaven, inlaid with living pearls,
And reached her hand up to her Father's.   Hark!
The thrilling music of God's welcome rang
Through all His eager host: "Arise, and shine!"

TO RUTH B———

On her Eleventh Birthday.

GROWN so much since first I knew thee!
Then a four-year-old so blue-eyed,
With thy winsome ways and trusting,
Round all hearts like tendrils twining.

Into wider fields of knowledge
Day by day on tiptoe peeping;
Like a rose with close-shut petals
Slowly opening to the sunlight.

Now a maiden full of comfort,
Kind, and happy, wise, and thoughtful;
Every year new graces adding,
Every day fond hopes fulfilling.

Blessed girl, thou hast a dowry
Richer than all mines and acres;
May the One thou callest Master
Know thee best as Ruth, his gleaner!

JUNE 13, 1893.

ON this day, the grateful climax
To the years of toilsome service,
As thou standest on the lookout
Searching e'en the far horizon,
With a friendly word I greet thee.

May the world, so wild and needy,
Find in thee a stanch apostle,
Bringing bread from God's own grain-mills,
And with trenchant blade and righteous
Pruning close the sprouts of evil.
And if need be, in His planning
That His cause may grandly triumph,
That a martyr He decrees thee,
Let thy courage not forsake thee,
Since His love thy soul hath tested.

Many a goal is still before thee;
But, however sweet and restful,
Or whatever thy advantage,
May it be but fresh beginning
In thy straight and sturdy progress
Toward the door of thine own mansion
Swinging wide on heaven's to-morrow!

THE BEGINNING OF HEAVEN.

(To S. S., translated March 11, 1894, five months after her wedding day.)

AND have thy sandals touched the golden floor?
Ah, me! the mile-stones looked so far and dim
Ahead, we almost thought thy feet and ours
Would evermore keep step; but here we stand,
And with unconscious awe look to the clouds,
The only way thou couldst have gone; with faith,
That fine-wrought telescope, we spy the gate
That swung wide open at thy soft approach.
But now 'tis shut and barred, with thee inside.

How farest thou, sweet friend, in thy new home?
Hast found thy Brother, and revealed Him all,—
The steep, rough way, the temptings, and the joy
And peace of prayer and His own comradeship?
Is't true, that thou canst look into His face,—
Those lustrous eyes, the vehicle of love,—
Whose very self is heaven's sufficient sun?
And doth the purple dusk ne'er settle down,
When weary angels drop their harps and sleep?

And hast thou met the Father? O, dear heart,
To feel the velvet touch of those kind hands,
And lean upon Him while He brushes off
All trace of tears! And in the Holy Book—
The promise which we live on who are left—
It tells of peace,—wide, deep, and perfect peace.
Dost sail upon that river? From the throne
It flows and dimples by the emerald banks
In low, sweet rhythm; and wilt thou ask the Lord
To make beside thee room for such as we?

162

Thou farest well, according to our hope!
Better than when, with comely virgin blush,
Thy hand thou gavest to the faithful friend
Whose arms protectingly enfolded thee
So briefly!   But he looketh upward now!
Of all the sweet beginnings of this life,
Of love, or hope, or glory, none can touch
The first glad moment in that upper zone
With song perennial girdled, and whose rest
Remaineth for God's own.   In heaven, hail!

A BIRTHDAY WISH.

(To W. F.)

WHILE young life breathes sweetness round thee,
    And God's gracious fingers lie
On thy brow,—with joy have crowned thee,
    Dread not gray November's sigh:
Only let this birthday find thee
    Pure, and true, and nobler grown;
May the vanished year remind thee
    Thou art nearer to His throne!

BEREAVED.

(To W. B. T.)

YE watchers grave,
What is't ye say? My mother dead?
Nay, crush me not with news so dread!
Her whose warm prayers e'er crowned my head
    Could ye not save?

The room is chill;
A shudder takes me, and I feel
The rush of phantom wings, which steal
Her spirit skyward; and I kneel
    Calling her still.

Oh, mother! pale
And pulseless are thy temples cold;
This shroud they made, with solemn fold,
Looks deathly; as thy hand I hold
    I read the tale.

My spirit brave
Sinks, smitten; oh, thou guide through years
Of childish sport and summer fears,
My heart weeps forth its manhood's tears,
    Wave after wave.

Mine earliest friend!
And truest, though the rest were kind,
Who for my sake to self wast blind,
Shall I again thy spirit find?
    Is this the end?

Not so; for love
Shall live eternal; and the choir
Of harps fresh-tuned shall voice the higher
Affection of the singers, nigher
    The throne above.

This comforts me:
Though orphaned here, my feet may stand
Some day with mother's and the band
Of angels on the shining strand
Beyond the sea.

IN THE MORNING.

(On the death of L. U., a student at College.)

MUFFLED voices paced the hallway,
Some one murmured, "She is dying!"
Heavy hearts and tear-wet eyelids
Spoke the grief for her who waited,
Waited with exalted gladness
For the coming of the Angel.

Night enfolded dome and campus—
Clung in still and starry robing;
Airs of spring outside her window
Fed fresh incense to her spirit
Reaching up to unseen glory.
Though unseen by all her schoolmates,
She, transfigured, saw it widen
Till the aisles of earth went merging
Into heaven's own sunny vistas,
And the shining ones came thronging
To take home their earth-born sister;
When she murmured, "O, sweet music!
I must go now; they are waiting."
Then warm hands their love imprinted,
Bent to hear her last monition:—

"Be ye priests in virtue's temple;
  Win a crown, and bring me tidings
  In the kingdom of our Father."
  Gloryward her eyes were lifted,
  Thus her last "Good-by!" was whispered.

"She is dead!"   O, skies benignant,
  Comfort now her weeping brothers!
  Gently calm her mourning sisters!
  Ye have answered; joy in trusting
  Now hath sanctified their sorrow,
  Brought to bloom a noble manhood,
  Set in pearls a woman's virtue.
  Night looped back her sable drapings,
  And the wheels of heavenly chariots
  Seemed to usher in the daybreak,
  All alight with love and promise:
  So the soul of her that's sleeping
  Took faith's journey in the morning!

TO A YOUNG FRIEND.

GOD has made thee woman:
    Dignify thy station;
  Bring to woman's altar
    Love's own ministration.

TRANSPLANTED.

(To Mr. and Mrs. E. A. Orr.)

ONE day a gentle angel
   Unbarred the gate of light,
Looked out upon the suburbs,
   And plumed his wings for flight.

The Sovereign of the heavens
   Commissioned him to bear
From out the royal gardens
   A rosebud frail and rare.

To earth he bent his journey
   And in a sheltered nook
He set the tiny floret,
   Beside a tuneful brook.

Two beings watched the planting:
   "Behold," the angel said,
"My Master makes you gardeners,
   To tend this in His stead."

With joy the charge was taken;
   And day by day were wrought
New wonders in the blossom,
   To which all care was brought.

The brooklet's sweet, low ripple
   The birds to music won;
But yet there hung a shadow
   Too dense for summer sun.

The petals pale and fragile
   Clung weakly to the stem;
The gardeners grew more tender
   Toward the fragrant gem.

All nurture proved but useless;
   With pain they read its fate,
When lo! the pale-winged angel
   Came in the garden gate.

"My Master needs this flower,"
   He said, with soothing grace,
Then laid it in his bosom,
   And turned to leave the place.

Thro' tears the gardeners watched him
   Climb up a beam of light;
He turned, and, smiling, showed them
   The flower grow fresh and bright.

Their strengthened eyes beheld him
   Replant it 'mid a spray
Of Sharon's royal roses,
   Where his Master loved to stray.

And then they bowed submissive
   Above the hallowed spot
Which once their hearts so tended,
   Where now the bloom was not.

TO GRACE F———.

THOUGH youth's pleasures have entwined thee,
   Seek thy jewels in the sky;
May thy gracious name remind thee
   Of the love for thee on high!

FLOWER-BEDS.

(Jennie Casseday, World's Superintendent Flower Mission, W. C. T. U., transplanted in the blossom season, 1893.)

CLOD after clod I turned up with my spade,
And every one a burrow, black and damp,
Of wriggling earthworms, squirming in the sun,
And twisting downwards toward the earth again.
I put some brown, hard seeds in those same clods,
And said, "Be still until the morrow break."
'Twas dawn, and day, and dusk; 'twas dawn again,
And sheaves of warm May light lay on the soil;
And there were quiet whispers 'mong the seeds:
"Let's up and take a survey by the sun;
This blanket's most too warm to stay in bed."
And presently there was a noiseless stir,
And soon a dozen dots of delicate green
Broidered the plain, black bed.   They climbed and
            spread,
And, like a maiden just from childhood stept,
Began to blush, like virgin snowdrifts brushed
With rosy dawn, and hid all sign of mold.
All summer long they nodded toward the road,
And shook their fragrance out, and many a foot
Would linger at the paling, to absorb
A share of beautiful blessing from my flowers.

Some men but burrow in the dens of self;
From black design hatch blacker progeny,
And all their thrift for sensuous ends but leaves
The earth a planet sunless, bare and dead.
But some—my soul springs up to wing the thought—
Some draw from soil of circumstance and time
The elements of life, and strength, and grace,
That top their manhood with a coronet
Of sweet-breathed blooms, that win all lookers-on

To reverent worship of their beauty, caught
From upper skies where August Goodness sits
In August loveliness. So bloomed a soul
Close-ranked with us till yesterday—a clear,
White lily, of a rarer strain than most
Who grow in corner-beds—now growing on,
More white, more pure, on God's own river-banks.
How much we joy in blossoms! and the earth
Might be a rose-field everywhere, if—*if*
We'd make it so. Like her that went away,
Do you, my comrade, steadily bloom, though tried ?

ADDRESS OF WELCOME

(To the W. C. T. U. County Convention at Huntingdon, Pa.,
Sept. 28, 1893.)

IN the name of our Jehovah,
He, the God of truth and mercy,
We are here in peace assembled
To receive fresh inspiration,
Hope and courage for the conflict
With the phalanxes of evil.

Strength is ever born of union;
So, with glad and hearty hand-clasp,
We, the members in this station
Of the great white-ribbon army,
Welcome you, our sister unions,
To the council of our camp-fire.

Brothers, aids-de-camp so trusty,
In an honest conscience stedfast,
On this common ground and sacred
We sincerely bid you welcome.
And to you we call outsiders

(Pity 'tis there is an outside
To the sphere of brave endeavor
To destroy the pitiless hydra
Nestling in our country's bosom)
Here we give the palm of welcome,
With a little prayer in it.

And the children, blessed hopefuls,
Quick in sympathy and reason
On this broad and burning question,
Planting, thro' their loyal legions,
Seed that in some mighty harvest
When their voice shall mould opinion,
Shall bring blessedness past hoping
To the thousands now in thralldom,—
Welcome, children, to this meeting.

Clear and thrilling from the border
Sound the drum-taps and the bugle,
Calling out reserve battalions
'Gainst the brazen-front Philistines.
Not a heart of us may quaver,
For the Lord of Hosts commandeth,
And with him, a loyal handful
Shall uprear the pure white banner
O'er the fallen leagues of darkness.

Long the cloven-footed monster
In a robe of legal ermine
Hath intrenched him and his allies
In the best homes of the nation,
And we've stood aghast and helpless,
Wondering oft, "How long, O Master?"
But there's yet a source availing,
Source of all the most unfailing,
Whence our armory may be furnished

With the truth's most trenchant weapons:
Message by electric cable
Flies not swifter thro' the ocean
Than dispatch from God's own finger
To our cry, "Send down and help us!"

All the powers that we inherit,
Gift of mind, or grace of temper,
Wealth, or beauty, strength, or influence,
We should consecrate to duty
In the battle of the moment.
In our serried ranks unflinching
Every face should flash one purpose—
"Down with trade forever sinful!—
Trade in souls, and tears, and heart-aches,
Trade that blots our nation's ensign,
Greatest that the pure sun shines on!"

Like a candle in the window
Of some lonely sea-beach dwelling,
May our separate lives keep shining
Out upon the waste, where hidden
Hungry reefs are nightly wrecking
Barks that long have lost their rudder,
Oar, and compass, and are floating
Like a seaweed toward the maelstrom.

As we watch the game stupendous
'Twixt the nation's statute-makers
And the home and conscience breakers,
With the drunkard as the foot-ball
Tossed at last in prison dungeon
For a crime themselves have breeded
Thro' the mocking wine that sparkles
In the vestibule of Hades,—
May a power that's more than human

Swiftly from the sky descending
Spur us to a mighty onset
'Gainst the forts of grinning license,
That no taunt of man shall baffle
But their bulwarks shall beleaguer
Till the citadel is taken,
And the flag of Prohibition
From its topmost tower be streaming!

God's in heaven, awake and strong-armed;
And all governments and peoples
Rise, or languish, as He beckons.
Whosoe'er His law defaces,
Be he potentate or pauper,
Sets himself a lone opponent
'Gainst the might of all God's angels.

Fear not, sisters; this Goliath,
In our eyes a foe so dreadful,
Shall not stand before the pebbles
Of an army of young Davids.
Fear ye not; our cause is righteous;
God has always kept His promise,
And His word shall surely prosper
In this work whereto He sends it.
Wear these words as gleaming frontlets
Day and night: "If God be for us,
Who in earth can stand againt us?"

DEDICATION

(Of a Western College Journal.)

WE come with the breath of the billowy prairie,
  The voice of the winds, with their soft southern
    balm,
With hands full of garlands and sheaves intertwining,
  To greet you, O people, with brotherhood's palm.

We come with the pennon of progress o'erstreaming,
  The image of wisdom embossed on our crest;
To art, toil and truth shall our front be devoted,
  With motto inspiring: "The highest and best."

We bring opportunity fresh and delightful
  To brains quick with genius and burnished with zeal;
We bear facts and wonders, survivors of ages,
  And stamp on the darkness enlightenment's seal.

We scatter the breezes of twin-peaked Parnassus,
  Attuned to the lyre with a heaven-born theme;
From lowlier granite we rear stately fabrics,
  The visible domes of an architect's dream.

We light with the glow of affection the hearth-stone
  And sprinkle with pleasure all homely employ;
Sweet peace, like the day, shall uprise from the shadows,
  And bind hearts and homes with a lingering joy.

New wisdom we offer the tiller of acres,
  To reap from his furrows a harvest of gold,
To pluck from his orchards, his gardens, and vineyards,
  The rarest perfections earth's treasuries hold.

We follow the artisan into his workshop,
  And turn into use fruits of mountain and mine;
On industries vast and performance domestic,
  We flash gleams of worthy and fertile design.

To dignify service, the people's uplifting,
　Our effort is pledged, our enthusiasm born;
We rise from the altar of our dedication,
　And sow on our journey the hopes of the morn.

DEDICATION

(Of the new Philorhetorian Society Hall, Mount Morris
College, Ill.)

K INDLE the altar, ye lovers of learning,
　　Pour on the incense of fealty's gift;
　Let its sweet vapors uprise thro' the temple,
　　And your pure prayers on its white wings uplift.

Think, as this court ye are eagerly thronging,
　At its one shrine ye are ministers all;
Bring to its service clean hands and white vestments,
　Free will unfeigned, tho' your offering be small.

Here let the pulse-beat of brotherhood quicken
　As ye tread softly this new hallowed ground;
Let our fair patroness, ever benignant,
　This day with honors new-burnished be crowned.

Faithful we've served thee and long, O Minerva,
　Tho' with small pomp has our homage been paid;
Fondly we call up those hopeful beginnings
　When our first humble foundations were laid.

Fame of thy wisdom drew by-passers nigh thee,
　Forthwith to pledge their allegiance to thee;
Soon we were crowds of devoted disciples
　Offering oblations on reverent knee.

Once, twice, and thrice has this altar been carried
  Into new shelter with rekindled zeal;
Now, as it finds fit abode in this sanctum,
  Fill each your censer, and pray for its weal.

Let these walls echo your orisons fervent,
  Tread ye unsandaled this consecrate floor;
Let the glad sound of your minstrelsy hover
  Like a spring fragrance the worshipers o'er.

Loyal to thee, O thou goddess of wisdom,
  Here we devote this new temple to thee;
Far hence let strife for dominion be banished,
  Each the true servant aspiring to be.

Now, as new duties and days are beginning,
  Plant round the altar-fire purposes new
That shall bear benefits broad and perennial,—
  Joy born of work and a charity true.

Stand fast a hero, O Philorhetorian!
  Let no dishonor e'er sully that name;
Only those souls can be great who are noble,
  Tho' all the nations might herald their fame.

TO MT. MORRIS COLLEGE.

On the Occasion of her Students' Reunion at Ottawa, Kansas,
May 26, 1896.)

UP from three coasts floats a concord of voices,
  Threading the States south and east, north and
    west,
Gathering its chorus from school-bell and plow-share,
  Blending in unison o'er the home-nest.

Fostering mother to glad generations!
  Still to thy skirts would thy loyal youth cling;
Scattered as destiny's winds may have blown them,
  Hover their spirits to-day 'neath thy wing.

Fountain of knowledge and great-minded purpose!
  Cradle of hope in God's brotherly plans!
Summit where faith, with its world-belting vision,
  Souls in the dark in deep sympathy scans.

Luminous center of righteous upbuilding!
  Spur of best impulses, sponsor of truth!
On the far beaches may harvests be springing
  From thy rich seeding, thy dowry of youth.

From the green strength of the minds thou dost nourish
  Blessing of bloom the dull world shall revive;
And with the salt of all honest endeavor
  Missions of eloquent virtue shall thrive.

Up let thy finger be pointing, our mother!
  Out from the crag show thine eaglets to fly;
So when our lowly careering we've compassed,
  We shall not fear the deep heavens to try.

A MILE-STONE.

(To the Eclectic Literary Society, Juniata College, on her
Twentieth Birthday, April 17th, 1896.)

A FATEFUL journey on the road of time!
'Twere good we rest a bit, and reinforce
Our drooping strength with reminiscent rhyme,
A gentle spur upon our starward course.

'Tis April now and morning for the throng
That at faith's tripod waits; cleft is the sky,
Tearful, yet blue, with peal of spring birds' song;
Hearts throb; hope builds;—pile the stern granite high!

As when the buds of oak and maple swell,
We look for early glimpse of emerald spray
Thick-set with blooms, and signs begin to tell
Of daisied valleys bringing in the May,
So the fresh youth, the laugh, the dewy eye,
The pride of mothers and of nature, bring
The promise of rare manhood by and by,
Whose fragrance of kind words and deeds shall swing
Like censers o'er the brown, dry fields of life.

Dawn of the mind! reason immortal, grand!
Helm of the hulk of life, for service great,
For riding o'er "a sea of troubles" planned,
On which all passions and temptations wait!

Here is the crowd; light-hearted some, and braced
With healthful exercise of sense and mind;
Some flushed and weary from the reckless waste
Of time spent chasing feathers on the wind;
A few stray laggards close the rear, and all
Press to one spot to count the years and deeds
Past and to come,—what fates and friends may fall
To each,—whether of laurel or of weeds
Their manhood's crowns may be;—they set a stone

To mark the place;—and whither now, O youth ?
The path is not all cleared yet; each his own
Hewing must do, nor look for comrade's ruth.
None may turn back; for by the fixed decree
Of heaven's high Infinite, every life must tend
Onward forever, whether grief or glee
Urge or dissuade,—on to the solemn end.

So to new pastures in the realm of thought,
And vineyards where the wine of wisdom grows
Bend your young feet; for never deeds are wrought
Worthy a man, save as his whole face glows
With highest reach of knowledge in his sphere,
With purpose grand, and utmost exercise
Of gift with which his God endowed him. Here
Pluck the full ears of learning; for the prize
Of truth in jewels overturn the soil
With shares thrice tempered by a pliant will
To mould to greatness all the petty toil
With book and pen, and fashion good from ill.

Life at its midday is a stern employ,
Needing all strength of mind and zeal of soul
Gathered in blossom-time, when life was joy
Mainly,—a sweet, brief prelude to the whole.
Enter the gates of noon with loving heart
As well as judging head; no ministry
So crowns a man with true, unconscious art
As loss of self in restless energy
To make wrong right, to brace the souls that faint,
To use his talent for the sake of God,
Distilling patience out of drear complaint,
Smoothing the road by tribulation trod.

To buy, and sell, and gain; to write a book;
To build a house, or sail upon the sea;

179

To play the master's music, or to cook;
To be well skilled in all the arts that be
Were poor attainment, if above it all
No sense of human brotherhood held sway
As pilot of the craft.   The words that fall
Like gracious rain-drops on an April day
Drop from the sky for you: the faithful tears
Which water other lives, nor guerdon ask,
Shall bring full harvest in the sunless years
Where God is light and love the only task.

SHUT IN.

(A reminiscence of the flood of 1889.)

ENDLESS the rain-sheets are pouring,
    Mournfully weeping the trees;
Yellow the flood in the river,
    Smothered the hum of the bees;
Zigzagged the slopes with mad torrents,
    Lakes on the flats where they meet;
Still o'er the sea of the heaven
    Sails the dun, mist-shrouded fleet.

Windows to eastward are streaming;
    Dim thro' their vista uprise
Mountains new-washed, with green foreheads,
    Beflowered with tender, wet eyes;
Spared not the clouds all the night-time,
    Ceased not their gift all the day;
Till, of the out-view aweary,
    Turns a wife slowly away.

Near lies a favorite poet,
    But in the rhythmical lines
Naught of the old life is flashing,
    Dimly his genius shines;

Closed is the dull, speechless volume;
  Greets the piano her eyes;
Idly she sits down before it,
  Waking its sweet, low replies.

Weighted the air seems around her;
  Spiritless murmur the strings;
Mocked by the rain's hollow drumming
  Round on the swift stool she swings,
Paces the room dark and lonely,
  Wonders the day is so void,
When at her hand lies the service
  Always her keen soul enjoyed.

Ah, 'tis her complement spirit
  On his first errand away
That has made this day a climax
  Over each other dull day.
Nothing will soothe but his presence,
  Naught for his smile compensate;
So, as she calls up his image,
  All else her mood must await.

Over the scene drops the darkness,
  Drenched with the ceaseless downpour;
Almost the clock-tick is silenced,
  Drowned in the storm's steady roar;
Tired of the hours long and laggard,
  Glad to her pillow she creeps,
Whispers a prayer to heaven,
  And dreams of her love as she sleeps.

        *   *   *   *   *

What of the lowlands by morning?
  When will the torrents be stayed?
Ah, hear the mad, rushing river!
  Swiftly its margins invade

Homes on their quiet green dotted,
　　Clasps in its wild hungry tide;
Cries of the desolate people
　　Check not the storm-spirit's ride.

Bowed to the earth are the grain-fields,
　　Crushed by such baptism of grief;
Flying and leaping the gulches,
　　Wrecking with carnival brief,
Gather the floods in the valleys,
　　Spurning all prayers in their track;
On sweeps the terrible besom,
　　Ne'er on its waste looking back.

God in His gracious foreknowing
　　Mete us some good from this rage!
Surely some creature must perish
　　Under the waters' wild wage;
Blessed the homes full of love-lights
　　Kindly untouched by alarms;
Praised be the name of the Father
　　Who keeps His beloved from harms.

IN THE AMPHITHEATER.

(A reminiscence of the Sunday service at Chautauqua, N. Y.,
July 27, 1890.)

A MORNING balm breathes thro' the sacred grove,
Where sunglints dally with the shy green leaves,
And trails of vapor put them all to blush.
Glad of the hour, and burdened with its strain,
The full voiced organ, with surchargèd pipes,
Trembles abroad, and calls God's worshipers.

Into their place are come ten thousand feet,
Gathered from climes 'neath every sun; the youth,
Decked with their summer bravery and smiles,
Next to the snow-strewn hair; the care-free child
The sainted sage beside; mothers and brides;
A sea of faces, cast in infinite mold.

"Who is my neighbor?" All these pulsing souls,
And all the world besides in need of help.
The beat of brotherhood vibrates across
Th' assembly, and a burst of loud "All hails!"
Leaps from all tongues, and round the rafters clings,
Dying in infinite waves far thro' the blue.

The sense of Fatherhood above the world,
That makes and holds and rules the peopled vast,
Thrills heart and song, and once again the swell
Of choral "Hallelujahs" shakes the air
In widening waves until the last broad crest
Breaks with sweet murmur on the shores of heaven.

O heaven, is this thy spectacle? Like this,
Do angels sing around the dazzling throne,
Source of thy light and rapture? O let me,
Gazing with tear-filled eyes at this earth-scene,
Mingle my quivering notes with that pure song
When this sweet memory shall cease to be.

AT GRACE.

(In the dining-room of State Normal School, West Chester,
Pa., April 21, 1889.)

THE Easter sun was nearing
　　The gateway of the west;
Its golden glints lay softly
　　Upon earth's holy rest;
Forth come to resurrection
　　Were grass, and leaf, and bloom,
And blithe young footsteps wandered
　　Thro' drifts of spring perfume.

The Easter peace stole gently
　　Within a spacious hall
Where hundreds sat at table,
　　And brooded over all;
With bowèd head and silent
　　Before the evening's dole,
Each sought his share of blessing
　　From God's gift-brimming bowl.

As passed the sacred moment
　　Unmarked by human word,
Forth burst upon the stillness
　　From a golden, cagèd bird,
A rippling storm of music
　　Pent in his songful throat,—
A tribute to his Maker
　　Voiced in his sweetest note.

Uprose his hymn like incense;
　　The wide room filled with praise,
And hearts of men and women
　　Blent on their heaven-bound ways;
O bird, of care unknowing,
　　Yet minister divine!
Teach us to know the Father,
　　And chord our songs with thine.

AT "CRYSTAL SPRING."

(One of the springs at Cresson, a mountain resort in the Alleghanies.)

To F. H. G.

THE dun clouds cover
    The autumn sky,
And wind-sprites hover
    The mountain nigh;
The woodland aisles are strewn with lifeless leaves,
And at our ruthless tread the forest grieves.

The prospect airy
    Our senses thrills,—
Fit for wood-fairy,
    Who life distils;
Sweet fern and daisies wild yet nod and smile
At frequent footstep; so we reach the stile.

A by-path leading
    Into retreat
Our guide is heeding
    With prompting feet;—
Here is the spot; we feel a sudden thirst;
Hither! and see who'll taste the fountain first!

The dead leaves litter
    The crystal wave;
Yet no draught fitter
    Wood-nymph e'er gave;
Nor cup nor green leaf's chalice does she bring,
But Guido quaffs, by handfuls, from the spring.

"Here's health and guerdon
    For toil and woe;
Fling off your burden
    And let joy flow!"

185

Alas! our gloves are laced too well, we fear;
But Guido becks, and smiles, and says, "Come here!"

Then stoop we laughing
    At that command,
The water quaffing
    From Guido's hand;—
Aha! how bounds the heart with happy life!
The very air with echoing joy seems rife.

The woodland spaces
    Seem dimmer now;
A nimbus graces
    The mountain's brow;
November's mood has changed; a falling mist
Grows into showers; come, rain-nymphs now hold
    tryst.

A DECEMBER MORNING IN ROCKDALE.

(A picturesque little glen near Bremen, Ohio, visited December
10, 1888.)

THE air is sweet and buoyant; scarce the frost
    Has whetted it; the dear old sun has donned
    A springtime air, and like a fairy wand
Reveals this witching grot, with gray rocks tossed
In cliffs and stairways, with green velvet mossed
    And fresh ferns mingled; pine and spruce respond
    In mellow madrigals to winds beyond
That visit here and are in music lost.

We ramble o'er the thick leaf-carpet sere,
  And all at once we hear a tinkling splash;
  We start in haste, and catch the silver flash
Of water trickling from a stone roof near.
The vault is wet and low, but to the rear
  We needs must clamber, while the slender dash
  Falls straight before us like a crystal sash,
Thro' which our friends like water-nymphs appear.

We start, and turn, and leave with lingering pace,
  And wander deeper in the mystic dale;
  When lo! the shimmer of a bridal veil
Sun-woven, takes our senses charmed; from base
To brow the modest cliff the sheeny grace
  Wears daintily; beside, in coat of mail,
  A swain with icy jewels decks his pale,
Sweet bride, and singing fairies throng the place.

A wall of rock arrests our further drift;
  The sun is high; we sigh, and turn away
  Regretfully, for such a radiant day
Is poet's luxury, the gods' rare gift.
We trace the outbound streamlet thro' the rift,
  And by its whispering purls we fain would stay;
  At last farewell!—be seasons green or gray,
This memory shall with joy our hearts uplift.

187

IX.

THE CHILD'S GARDEN.

THE CHUMS.

AMONG the shady shrubs and trees,
  In blue and golden weather,
And up and down the sunny path,
  Content they stroll together.

Above the highest leafy tops
  They watch the song birds skimming,
And in the pond, so still and clear,
  The sportive minnows swimming.

The elder she by some eight years,
  Her face in frankness moulded;
A rare pink bud, with future charms
  Deep in her soul enfolded.

A prattler he of summers three,
  With deep brown eyes and dancing;
All things obscure they quickly spy,
  Like morning sunbeams glancing.

Such confidences as they have!
  His short arms round her clinging,
"I like you, Ruth," he sweetly says,
  A hug responsive bringing.

With play he mingles scraps of hymns,
  His infant lips confessing
To "Jesus, lover of my soul,"
  And "Fount of every blessing."

"Now, Leon, let's play 'hide and seek' ";
  So in a corner cosy
They peep, and laugh, then gaily run,
  And "ring a round a rosy."

No quarrel ever wrecks their glee,—
  So innocent it bubbles;
O, Father, tide them safely o'er
  The shoals of earthly troubles!

BONNIE BELL.

"I'LL sing you a little song,"
  Said bonnie Bell one day;
"It won't be very long,
  So listen what I say.

"You musn't make a noise,
  Nor whisper while I sing,
For only naughty boys
  Would do so rude a thing."

So our dainty, dimpled girl,
  All dressed in pink and white.
Head flossed with many a curl,
  Stood like a fairy bright.

Her eyes, long fringed and blue,
  So deep they held the sky,
Like violets dipped in dew
  Shone in her glances shy.

We watched her mouth so small,—
  Twin rose-leaves just apart;
We hardly breathed at all,
  Waiting to hear her start.

"When I was out at play,
  I saw a little bird;
And he called across the way,
  'Sweet maiden, have you heard?

" 'We birds have formed a band
  To sing the summer through:
We'll visit all the land,
  And bear a message true.

" 'We'll stop at hovels poor
  Where sick ones lie in pain,
And crowd about the door
  And make them glad again.

" 'We'll wake the world at morn
  With comfort for the day;
We'll make men cease to scorn,
  And drive bad thoughts away.

" 'We haste our work to do
  Ere winter skies are here;
And will you help us true,
  O sunny maiden dear?' "

Ah, Bell, your little song
  Is sweeter than the bird's;
To angel harps belong
  Such soft and tinkling words.

Bright messenger of peace!
  Where'er your face appears,
Hard feelings quickly cease,
  And joy replaces tears.

Long may you live to fill
  The world with better things,
Before your soul grows still,
  And leaves us with white wings.

APPLE-TIME.

SING a song of apple-time!
  Yellow, green and red,
How they peep among the boughs,
  Drooping overhead!
Down the lane comes whistling John,
  Basket swinging high;
Now we'll have some jolly fun,
  Johnny, you and I.

Here's a bushel, maybe more,
  On the nearest tree;
Like a squirrel John runs up,
  First-class shaker he;
Such a shower comes thumping down,
  Golden pippins rare;
Hold your hat, your apron, too;
  See! they're everywhere.

Now we'll gather some for John;
  Pile the basket high;
They'll be fine when winter comes
  And the snowflakes fly.

Now let's shake this other tree
Where the red-streaks glow;
Bravo! fill your lap again;
Aren't they juicy, though?

What a feast is apple-time
In the orchard gay!
Sweeter now the ripened fruit
Than the blooms in May.
Let us thank the Giver good
For such wondrous store;
Where we go His tender love
Follows evermore!

ROSE AND HER LAMBS.

"MARY had a little lamb,"
The ancient story goes;
But once I knew another girl,
And people called her Rose.

Her father had a merry flock
Of lambkins, black and white;
And out of these, two special pets
She guarded day and night.

She fed them with her own small hand
Sweet bits of tender grass;
And round her feet they gaily skipped
Whene'er they saw her pass.

One day, beneath a sturdy oak
Her woolly pets were laid
To rest them from their frolics wild
Beneath its cooling shade.

Her lessons learned, young Rose went out
  To rest her, too, awhile;
She spied her lambs not far away,
  And quickly crossed the stile.

They sprang to greet her as she came;
  She smiled, and stopped to say,
"What have you done, my snow-white dears,
  To pass the time away?"

They did not tell her, for you see
  They never went to school
To learn to speak and write their thoughts
  And break the teacher's rule.

They were a happy set, the three,
  Thro' all the summer days,
And Rose grew gentler as she learned
  Her lambkins' pretty ways.

CHRISTMAS DAWN.

'TWAS a starlit, frosty time
  (As the stories tell in rhyme)
When two young and dreamful heads
Snuggled in their downy beds;
Stockings dangled here and there
Gorged to shapes so queer and square;
Stillness filled the little room
In the early Christmas gloom.

Lo! to eastward springs the day,—
Palest pink on sheets of gray;
Then a mellow, golden glow
Rims the darkness from below;
Now a point of sparkling light
Leads the warm, broad sun in sight;
And each little sunbeam trips
O'er those rosy, sleeping lips.

Beryl was the first to wake;
Gave herself a little shake;
"My! it's Christmas, brother dear!"
Then she whispered; "don't you hear?"
Quickly showed the round, blue eyes,
Clear and deep as summer skies;
"O, I 'member! 'twas a goose
I was dreaming 'bout," said Bruce.

"After waiting one whole year,
Aren't we glad—O, just look here!"
Out upon the coverlid
Fell the wealth so poorly hid;
Noah's ark, and jumping-jack,
Top, and whip with merry crack;
Picture-book, and dainty doll,
Red tin horse, and—that's not all.

Nuts, and candies red and white,
Oranges—a golden sight—
Thoughts of love with every toy
Brimmed their little hearts with joy.
"O, it's just the loveliest day!"
Beryl cried; "I think some way
We should thank our friends so true."
"Yes," said Bruce, "I think so too."

197

MAMA'S MERRY HELPERS.

O

N a sloping, sunny roof,
  In the August weather,
Madge and Dick—a happy pair—
  Conned their book together;
With her arm about his neck,
  He upon her leaning,
Dick picked out the pictures first,
  Madge explained their meaning.

"Here's a boy 'bout big as me,"
  Dick said, leafing over;
"There's his dog, with curly tail;
  'Spect his name is Rover."
Madge spelled out the letters tall—
  "Dick's the boy's name, truly!
Well, he looks some like you, too;
  But the dog's name's 'Coolie.'"

Now and then they stopped to laugh
  At the funny places.
Presently the dipping sun
  Shone right in their faces.
"My, it's almost supper-time!
  Come, else mama'll wonder
If her chicks have gone to roost
  'Fore the sun was under."

Gaily from the roof they slid,
  On the soft grass landing;
At the kitchen door they found
  Their dear mama standing.
"O, we've had a lovely time!"
  Both exclaimed together;
"Now we'll bring some water fresh;
  This is such warm weather."

WHAT CAME OF THE RACE.

ONE December afternoon,
'Neath a sky as fair as June,
With the barnyard all a-tune,
    Guy suggested,
"Since to-morrow's Christmas day,
I propose some lively play;
Let's run down old 'Gobble' gay,
    Proud and crested.

"He has lived 'bout long enough;
Soon he'll get so stiff and gruff
I'm afraid he'll be too tough
    To be eaten."
"I'm agreed," was Clem's reply;
"I remember once when I
Chased the scamp and left him by,
    Badly beaten."

Mother watched them "set their stakes,"
Mixing dough for Christmas cakes
(Sovereign cure for boyish aches
    She knew fully);
Soon a flutter and a flight
Round the snowy hay-stack white
Told the race was at its height,—
    Rousing, truly.

Through the garden gate they rush,
Through the briery berry brush,
And each handy patch of slush
    Headlong bounding;
Toward the kitchen door they turn,
Guy and Clem with faces stern,
"Gobble" full of great concern,
    Fears confounding.

"Head him off there, mother, quick!
I 'most had him, but he's slick!
Now he's off for 'nother trick,"
    Both boys grumbled;
Round the corner like a flash
Flew a tail; with one blind dash
Guy reached after; with a crash
    Flat he tumbled.

Then for laughing Clem stood still;
"My! but wasn't that a spill?
Guess old 'Gobble' has his will
    Once more, hain't he?"
But Guy shook his strength together;
"Guess a fellow's legs ain't leather,
But I'll pluck him, every feather,
    Clean and dainty."

Set upon by triple foe,
Floundering in a pile of snow,
"Gobble's" glory now lay low
    Once he boasted.   *   *   *   *
Christmas diners peeped about
As the oven door swung out,
Drowned the air with merry shout,
    "Now he's roasted!"

SWINGING ON THE GATE.

OVER the old farm-gate
   Lads and lassies gay,—
Heads of flax and auburn—
   Clamber in their play;
On the top rail balanced
   Davie shouts with glee;
See! his head 'most reaches
   To the maple tree.

John's so queerly twisted,
   Legs and rails entwined;
Daisy laughs, her ringlets
   Flying out behind;
Charlie's kicked his shoes off
   (They're too warm, you know),
And he swings the old gate
   Gaily to and fro.

Tot, alas! from glory
   On the green grass fell;
Whether laughing, crying,
   You could hardly tell;
Dash, with aimless bounding
   Helps the fun along;
And the orchard echoes
   With the mirth and song.

Sunny days of childhood,
   Free from care and fret!
When the world grows gloomy,
   You are precious yet;
We shall all remember,
   Though we live till late,
How we once went swinging
   On the old farm-gate!

AT A TEA-PARTY.

SAID Florence to Ruth, "Let's play
    We'll visit and stay to tea!
I'll ask you to come over first,
    And after that you'll ask me.

"Of course we'll take dollies along,
    Your Fay and my sweet little Queen;
With our tea and our talking we'll have
    The loveliest time ever seen!"

So out from the bureau drawer
    They lifted the dainty girls
With dresses of pink, gold, and blue,
    And beautiful, sunshiny curls.

All's ready; the tea-table's set,
    And carefully tidied the floor;
The hostess looks fresh as a peach,
    When hark! there's a rap at the door.

"My dear Mrs. Simpkins, come in!
    You haven't been here for a week;
And dear little Fay, is she well?
    Queen's hoarse, so she hardly can speak."

"We're well, thank you, dear Mrs. Flynn;
    Too bad little Queenie's been sick;
I was 'fraid I'd have trouble with Fay,
    But I dressed her up warm and thick.

"This tea is delicious, indeed!
    Pray, where do you buy this brand?
There, Fay, do not muss up your dress;
    Take your spoon in the other hand."

"O, my husband keeps store, you know,
    And we always get the best.
Did you hear Mrs. Jenks's boy
    Has gone to the far, far west?

"They say he's so wild,—oh, dear!
    Whatever'll the poor woman do?
Do have some more biscuit and tea;
    O, surely you are not through?"

"O, yes, you've so many good things,
    I really can't taste any more.
I think that new collar of Queen's
    The prettiest ever she wore.

"Now, dear Mrs. Flynn, we must go;
    Remember to come over soon;
The lily's just ready to bud
    You gave me, you know, last June."

"Indeed, Mrs. Simpkins, I will;
    You make such *beautiful* pie;
Now you 'member and come soon again."
    "Yes, thank you, I will.   Good-by."

THE CATS AND THE MONKEY.

ONCE there were two hungry cats
  (So the fable goes);
When they found a slice of cheese,
  High dispute arose.
How to share the lucky find
  They could not agree;
So they called a monkey in
  Upright judge to be.

"Let me see," he wisely said,
  Picking up the prize;
"I must break it first in two
  Parts of equal size.
To be sure one weighs no more,
  Nor the other less,
Here, I'll put them in the scales:
  Ah, I've missed my guess.

"See, they do not balance well;"
  So, with justice bold,
From the larger piece he bit
  All his mouth would hold;
Now the scale was much too light;
  So, to make it true,
From the other side he munched
  Till it flew up too.

"Hold!" exclaimed the hungry cats;
  "We shall lose our meal."
But the judge kept weighing cheese,
  Deaf to their appeal.
"This last morsel," then said he,
  Stowing it away,
"Is my fee to judge this case.
  Court's dismissed. Good-day."

He who right and justice seeks
   Must not go to law;
Fools are they who trust their gain
   To a monkey's paw.

MY PUSSY.

SEE my pussy sleeping sound!
Like a snowball white and round;
But his fur is soft and sleek
Like a peach's velvet cheek;
Round his neck a ribbon blue
Here and there is peeping through;
He is dreaming this warm day;
Pretty pussy, wake and play!

See him twitch his small, pink ears!
Wonder if my call he hears?
Now he opens one bright eye—
Mischief in its blink I spy!
Bounds he from his cosy place,
Rubs his whiskers 'gainst my face,
Talks to me with knowing purr,
While I stroke his silky fur.

Off he scampers for my ball,
Under sofas, through the hall,
Holds it tightly with four paws,
Round his legs the tangle draws;
Then he straightens up so prim,
And I sit and laugh at him;
Such a pet you never knew:
Don't you like my pussy too?

THE WHISTLER.

I HAVE a bright-eyed neighbor boy
   Who rises every morning
To catch the earliest peep of day,
   And gives his jolly warning;
I cannot sleep another wink,
   So out at last I scramble;
But those glad notes still follow me
   In all my daily ramble.

No matter if the sun is hot,
   And weeds are tall and spiteful,
His willing hoe speeds nimbly on,
   That whistle is delightful;
And when at eve the barnyard train
   Their homeward way are wending,
That whistle gay brings up the rear,
   With cow-bells softly blending.

And when the north wind drives the snow,
   And pipes his winter warning,
My neighbor laughs at such a voice
   And such a freezing morning;
Across the glassy lake he glides,
   Or on his sled goes flying;
And all the hills that whistle catch,
   With echo sweet replying.

WINTER SONG.

CUDDLE close, my baby dear,
For the frosty king is here;
How he whistles at the door,
Blows his breath across the floor;
Here he comes to warm his toes
Where the merry wood-fire glows;
Come, we'll chase him quickly back:
Hear the stirred-up fagots crack!

We are cosy, Gretchen dear,
Though the outside world is drear;
Here's our supper by the fire,
Fit for duke or even higher;
Toast and milk so fresh and fine,
Such a bowlful, baby mine!
Lets begin our royal fare;
Such gift falls not everywhere.

Some are out this star-cold night,
Watching sadly windows bright;
Heaven protect their freezing feet,
Give some crumbs that they may eat;
Sweet my baby, you are warm,
Safe from icicle and storm;
While the shades around us creep,
Come, I'll croon you, dear, to sleep.

THE NINE O'CLOCK BELL.

LISTEN, children, don't you hear it
   Ringing on the morning air?
'Tis the time when merry youngsters
   Gather here from everywhere;
Bringing cheeks and lips like roses,
   Dancing eyes of many a hue,
Spirits light and minds determined
   Every solemn task to do.

     Ding! dong! ding! dong!
  Now the flock comes trooping in;
     Ding! dong! ting-a-ling!
  That's the signal; work begin.

Shine and summer, clouds and winter,
   Speaks the old bell's faithful tongue,
Calling up to heights of knowledge,
   Calling ever to the young:
"Hither turn your happy footsteps,
   Pearls of truth lie hidden here;
Light, and power, and joy, and wonder,
   Wait for those who persevere."

When our school-days all are numbered,
   Shall we e'er forget the sound
Of that worn, familiar clapper
   Calling us the seasons round?
Ah, if we shall come to honor,
   If the world our works shall tell,
We'll be glad for childhood struggles,
   We will bless the old school bell.

THE PATTER ON THE PANES.

UPON the fresh'ning western breeze
    A shadow rises fast;
The birds have ceased their concert wild,
    And men go hurrying past;
A drop is dashed upon the glass,—
    Another—and yet more;
And now they come in bucketfuls,
    With what a splash and roar!

        Drip, dash, pour!
        There's music when it rains;
    A song is falling from the sky
        And patters on the panes.

The trees are eager for the shower,
    And lift their dusty crown
To gather in each leafy cup
    The drink that's pouring down;
The grass is brightening by the road,
    The flowers are happy too,
And nod, and blink the drops away
    And shed their fragrance new.

The meadow brooks are running o'er,
    And lave the patient feet
Of gentle flocks that browse content
    In pasture clean and sweet;
From hill and mead, from wood and town,
    The grateful tokens rise
For crystal showers that carry life
    And blessing from the skies.

HOW MARCIA FOUND THE WAY.

ALONG the road young Marcia came,
 On loving errand bent;
With scraps of song she trudged her way,
 With daisies thick besprent;
A generous basket on her arm,
 A tin pail full of cheer,
She said, "How sweet is all the world,
 With flowers and brooks so near!"

Then to the woods young Marcia came,
 When, to her startled eyes,
A great, white shepherd dog ran out
 And spoke, to her surprise:
"Dear maiden, see yon warning sign;
 Pray to your steps take heed;
If you will trust me as your guide,
 The way I'll safely lead."

Upon the tree young Marcia read
 Of "Highway Robbery;"
With frightened look she turned about
 And minded her to flee;
But braver thoughts sprang up full soon;
 She answered cheerily:
"Good dog, I'll venture on, if you
 Will bear me company."

So through the woods young Marcia went,
 With escort strong and true;
Once in the deepest shade she heard
 A night-owl's weird "boo-hoo!"
And once a flock of crows flew past
 In noisy, cawing mood;
But all unharmed the pair came forth
 From out the robbers' wood.

Then Marcia bade her friend good-bye,
　　And hastened on her way.
"How brave you were, my little dear!"
　　Said crippled Grandame Gray.
"O, when I thought that I must come
　　Because my duty led,
And that no harm befalls the good,
　　'Twas easy," Marcia said.

COASTING.

HEIGHO!　Here we go
With a dash and a bound o'er the frost-bitten snow;
　　Steer straight, jolly mate,
As we fly down the hill at this wonderful rate.

　　Drive care!　as we fare
With a light, tinkling laugh thro' the cool, brac-
　　ing air;
　　Glad we!　joy is free;
Far away may the troubles of yesterday flee.

　　Heigho!　stopping so?
Then again to the top trudge we cheerily, O!
　　Hooray!　this is gay;
May our lives brighter be for the sport of to-day.

THE DEMON-KING.

THERE'S a demon in the land,
　　　Have a care!
And he rules with cruel hand,
　　　O, beware!
Cunningly he becks and smiles,
With fair promises beguiles,
Till your honor he defiles;
　　　O, beware!

On the highway swift he roams,
　　　Have a care!
Rudely shatters peaceful homes,
　　　O, beware!
Like a spider in his den,
Merrily calls, and calls again,
Thirsting for the souls of men;
　　　O, beware!

All your lands and goods he takes,
　　　Have a care!
Of his servants fools he makes,
　　　O, beware!
Dearest links he breaks apart,
Tramples on your mother's heart,
Stabs the pure with ruthless dart,
　　　O, beware!

O'er the walls of truth he leaps,
　　　Have a care!
In the halls of justice creeps,
　　　O, beware!
Rich and poor before him fall;
Worse than death his iron thrall;
Mighty scourge, King Alcohol!
　　　O, beware!

Up and at this monstrous foe,
        Do not spare!
With your ballot lay him low,
        Nobly dare!
Strike, with word and prayer and deed,
Till our fatherland is freed;
Strike! your God and mercy plead;
        Strike, nor spare!

A SONG OF THE COUNTRY.

HURRAH! for the sunny green meadows,
    The blue laughing sky overhead;
The brooks 'neath the silvery willows,
    The daisies that border their bed.

Hurrah! for the spring full of blossoms;
    The ride on the new, fragrant hay;
The wealth in the yellowing grain-fields,
    The charm of the birds' morning lay.

Hurrah! for the orchards and vineyards
    That bend with their exquisite load;
The nuts in the heart of the woodland,
    The berries that blush by the road!

    Three cheers for the country!
    Its pleasures so bonny and rare;
Queen Nature reclines in these bowers,
    And bids us her happiness share.

DOROTHY AT THE TELEPHONE.

HELLO! dear Mr. Editor,
   Who live so far away,
And little reader boys and girls,
   How are you all to-day?

My dolly's tired, and so am I,
   At keeping house, you know;
We've washed the dinner dishes clean,
   And set them in a row.

I think I'll put her soon to bed
   To take her daily nap;
And then I'll read my "Daniel" book,
   With pussy on my lap.

You haven't seen my kitty yet;
   Well, I just wish you could;
So woolly, white, and soft he is,
   And so polite and good.

My papa's gone away to-day,
   'Way down past Walnut Creek;
For he's a doctor, and you know
   So many folks are sick.

My mama's just the sweetest girl;
   She laughs and romps with me,
And shows me how to sew and sweep,
   And set the plates for tea.

So many things I have to learn
   And so we play at school;
And every day she teaches me
   Besides, the Golden Rule.

I'd like to have you visit us,
  And taste my mama's pie;—
My dolly's nodding; I must go;
  So, gentle folks, good-by!

A WHEELBARROW IN JUNE.

SUCH a green and glorious day!
  Dews and violets of May
Changed their daintiness full soon
For the roses red of June;
Meadows look like flower-beds,
Red and white with clover-heads;
Faintly tinkling bells are heard
With the song of breeze and bird.

Gardens glow with sunlight gay,
Children on the soft grass play;
O'er the lawn, in merry chase,
Now they skip with rosy face;
Soon the gardener's tools they spy
As they on the barrow lie;
"Heigho, Daisy! want a ride?
I can wheel it, cause I've tried."

In she climbs, our Daisy sweet,
Hanging out her chubby feet;
Molly grasps the handles wide,
Tries the wiggling wheel to guide;
Merrily down the path they go,
And the sunbeams brighter grow;
For their hearts are glad, you see;—
There's a thought for you and me.

TO ———.

WHEN the years have made thee woman,
  May thy memory recall
Naught but goodness in thy childhood,
  Love and pity shown to all.

TO A LITTLE GIRL.

BE a merry beam of sunshine,
  Be a lily pure and fair;
Be a jewel bright and precious,
  Be a maiden good and rare.

216